PF

The Princess Fables

Stories
by
Marc Clark

Illustrations
by
Eric Hosford

D1444875

Edited by Maria.. _____

ISBN 978-0-9910345-0-5
WGAW Registration Number: 1666765

For Taylor...

"I believe that you are... and always will be... my little princess."

A Little Princess by Frances Hodgson Burnett

The Fables

Introduction   page 4

The Princess Who Always Said
   "I Don't Wanna'"   page 5

The Princess Who Always Said "No"   page 13

The Princess Who Wouldn't Wake up   page 25

The Princess Who Always Said "Not Today"   page 35

The Princess Who Hid Under The Covers   page 43

The Princess Who Never Let Go   page 51

The Princess Who Was Too Scared   page 61

The Princess Who Never Spoke   page 69

The Princess Who Always Said "Please"   page 79

The Princess Who Grunted   page 89

The Princess Who Always Said "Hey"   page 99

Introduction

I'm not big on introductions so I'll make it quick.

When our daughter was just beginning the first grade, she was not happy about school. She told me with tears in her eyes, "They make me learn, all day!," so she really didn't want to get out of bed in the morning. When I would come to wake her, I would kiss her chubby cheek or run my hand through her soft curls. Whatever her first response would be - and it was usually something to try to get out of having to go to school – that would be my subject for a Princess Fable.

If she'd say, "I don't want to," I'd make up a tale about The Princess Who Always Said, "I Don't Wanna'." If she clamped her mouth shut and refused to say a word, I'd tell her the story of The Princess Who Never Spoke. By the end of each Fable I'd have her dressed and ready for school, with her eyes wide open and full of hope for what the day might bring.

I wrote these stories down as well as I could remember them in the hope that another parent could tell them to another Princess who might need a little encouragement… or a reason to believe in happy endings.

The Princess Who Always Said, "I Don't Wanna'"

PF

Once there was a peaceful kingdom with a lovely castle overlooking the ocean. The King and Queen were very good to their subjects and were loved by all.

There were two little Princesses in the kingdom. The youngest had curly red hair and freckles. She was as bright as a shiny new button and her name was Katie.

Although, on the surface, she was a sweet little girl, Princess Katie had developed one not-so-pretty habit of saying, "I don't wanna'." It was sort of funny when she was very young, say three or four years old. That pudgy, freckly face staring up at you made almost anything she said sound cute and harmless but as the years went on, it got less and less adorable until it became rather annoying.

Since everyone in the castle was very nice they put up with this not very attractive habit, - somehow that made it even worse.

Princess Katie just kept saying, "I don't wanna'," to more and more stuff.

"I don't wanna' learn to sail."

"I don't wanna' learn to swim."

And even, "I don't wanna go outside the castle!"

Now, as you can imagine, this kind of behavior couldn't last forever before something bad happened.

Well, it happened when the rains came.

It had never rained so hard and so long. Up against the sea and with a river behind them, a lot of the kingdom and especially the castle were slowly being flooded.

Everyone pulled together to build walls to keep out the floodwaters that rose from the river but the rain just wouldn't stop. The King and his advisors decided that they would have to help everyone across the river to higher ground. Because they lived by the sea, they had all the boats they needed.

The King's men came to get the Princesses and the Queen first but, of course, Katie said, "I don't wanna'."

The Queen was furious and was going to have her dragged from the castle but Jennifer, Katie's older sister said she'd stay with her and get her onto another ship.

The soldiers then took the old and the feeble, went on to the women and children and finally they gathered the rest of the men. Those who lived in the castle were the last to go and, again, when it came time for the Princesses to get on a boat Katie said, "I don't wanna'."

I know, you'd think that's a stupid thing to do, right? What was she going to do instead, stay and drown? But there's something you should know about people, especially kids: when they're really afraid, they sometimes act angry - mostly so that nobody can tell that they're scared.

It was true for Katie. Most of her "I don't wanna's" were because she was afraid to do them.

And now she was really, REALLY scared. So when her Nursemaid gathered all of Katie's things together and said, "Princess, it's time to go," Katie clutched her knees to her chest in her huge, fluffy bed and said, "I don't wanna'."

The Nursemaid tried to reason with her. She explained that her own family was already ashore and that there was no time left, but Katie still said, "I don't wanna'."

The Nursemaid was frightened, too. If it had been her own daughter she would have grabbed her and dragged her to the boat, kicking and screaming, but this was a Princess so she couldn't. So, she tried again to talk to Katie.

"Katie," she said desperately, "staying here is dangerous. We could drown. You could die. No one is allowed to stay. You have to come and you have to come now."

And what do you think Katie said? "I don't wanna'."

The Nursemaid burst out in tears. She cried, "My own children, my family, will perish if we don't go now, your highness. Please come with me."

Katie, more afraid then ever said, "I don't wanna'."

The Nurse went to Princess Jennifer for help. Jennifer said, "I'll take care of it, Nurse. You look to your family now."

Jennifer brought along soldier after soldier as she walked down the hallway. By the time they got to Katie's room she had a half-dozen men behind her.

"Katie," she said to her frightened little sister, huddled in her pillows, "I and my soldiers will protect you from whatever harm may come… Will you join us, sister?"

"I don't wanna'," Katie said, crying.

"I know, little one. I know. I don't want to either. But I will... because I am a Princess, the daughter of a King, as you are, and we must have the courage to do what others will not."

Jennifer held out her hand to her little sister... finally Katie took her sister's hand and they left the castle together.

They were true and brave soldiers and seamen aboard the ship and it took all of their talent and all of their bravery to make the journey. The river had disappeared completely by now - it was all raging sea around the castle. It was more frightening than little Katie - or any of them - had ever imagined. There were waves that washed over the boat and almost took them under. There was lightening that almost blinded them and thunder that pounded in their ears.

When they finally came close to the shore the ship was thrown against the rocks by a huge wave and everyone on board was tossed into the sea.

Most of the crew and passengers were washed toward shore but Katie and some others ended up in the water, heading out to sea.

Katie went down, under the water, for the first time in her life. She kept going down and down. Somehow she ripped off her heavy dress and immediately floated to the surface. She caught her breath and grabbed at a floating piece of wood. It turned out to be the long boat that had been tied to the back of the ship. It was turned over and since she couldn't get it upright she held on until it floated to the rocks. She climbed out of the water in her bloomers, sat on the rocks and coughed up water.

As she looked out over the stormy sea, she could see large waves coming right at her. She scrambled up the slippery rocks as fast as she could as the waves pounded at her feet. She kept climbing because she knew the only way to get to the shore was to climb over the rocky cliff.

That's when she heard a cry. It sounded like a young boy. The voice came from below her. She climbed down a little bit and saw the Nurse's son huddled on a shelf in the rocks, crying. He was only a couple of years younger than she was - maybe four or five.

She couldn't get to the boy but she reached out to him and cried, "Grab my hand, I'll pull you out. You have to come with me."

"I don't wanna'," he cried.

The Princess looked far off into the ocean and saw another huge wave forming. "It'll be okay. I'll help you. But you have to get out now. A wave is going to come and take you out to sea!"

"I don't wanna'," he cried.

Katie turned back to the swelling wave. "Please take my hand!" she begged the boy.

"I don't wanna'!" he cried.

Katie's face became hard and she yelled at the crying boy, "I don't care what you want or don't want! I am your Queen! You do as I say and take my hand this instant!"

The boy's hand shot up immediately.

The Princess grabbed it and pulled him up with all of her might. He wrapped his arms around her neck. She held him in one arm and pulled herself up the rocky cliff as fast as she could.

She screamed as the huge wave pounded the rocks. She covered the boy's head and ducked down as water poured over them and giant pieces of shattered wood from the long boat landed all around.

She got right back up and pulled them both up the cliff and out of the water as the wave subsided. She didn't stop until she got to the very top. She tried to set the Nurse's son down but he wouldn't release his little arms from around her neck. So she carried him down the other side of the rocks to the beach.

Soldiers, seamen and the Nurse all came running as Princess Katie crossed the sandy beach toward the refugees.

The Nurse's son refused let go of the Princess' neck, even when his mother tried to take him in her arms. "She saved me! She saved me!"

The Nurse couldn't help herself, and she hugged them both together and kissed them both together and she thanked Katie over and over as she cried all over both of them.

At last the boy let go and snuggled into his mother's arms. The soldiers covered the Princess with a warm blanket and led her to her older sister who was caring for the injured.

Jennifer saw her and ran to her. The Princesses hugged each other and laughed and cried. Jennifer said to her little sister, "Do you want to get on some warm clothes and maybe have some soup?"

And through her smiling tears Katie said, "I really wanna'."

THE END

The Princess Who Always Said, "No"

$\mathcal{PF}$

Once upon a time, long, long ago, in a Kingdom really far away from your house a beautiful Princess was born. Everyone said she was the loveliest child they'd ever seen. Kings and Queens from other kingdoms oooh'd and aaah'd over her. And her parents just knew that she'd be the most perfect child in the world.

But you have to be careful about what you think you know until you know it for sure, because the Princess - her name was Julia by the way – wasn't quite as perfect as everyone had hoped. Actually, she didn't turn out to be very nice at all.

It all started when she said her very first word: "No." Now, let's be fair, a lot of times a child's first word is "No," because that's what they hear mostly when they're little: "No, don't do this. No, don't do that. No, put that down. No, take that out of your mouth." That kind of thing. But this wasn't that kind of thing. It didn't sound like that kind of thing. It wasn't mommy saying, "No, baby, don't cry." It wasn't a daddy's firm but worried, "No, don't put your finger in there," or an Aunt's, "No, you don't, you little schmookems."

Julia's "No" was different. It was a spoiled, pouty kind of "No," that had to be said with a twist of her head. The "N" was a little longer, the "O" was a little shorter, and it sounded like she put a "y" in it, too. So it sounded more like, "Nnyo." It was kind of a nasty, rude little "No," and people didn't like it. Not one bit. Because for Julia – and this is important - "No" meant "No!"

It doesn't matter how many times parents say, "No means No," one of the first things a child learns is that that's not true. "No," doesn't always mean "No," at least not when it comes from a grown up. Mom might say, "No, you can't have that." But if you ask her a few more times or ask really nicely or say you'll clean your room or help set the table, there's a good chance she'll say, "Yes." And if Dad says, "No, baby, not right now. Daddy has work to do," you can crawl into his lap and snuggle up to him and, sooner or later, there's bound to be an "Oh, alright, but just this once." Now, you kind of have to admit that when little girls are still very little and round and super cute and their hair is all curly and their cheeks are chubby and on top of all that they really are princesses… well they're usually cute even when they're saying, "No." But this doesn't last.

Then, when they get older and their "Nos" take on a little more weight and a little more power, the cuteness of it all kind of gets drained away. Well, that's what happened.

What else happened was that it became very difficult to teach Julia anything because if she got it into her mind that she didn't want to learn – she just plain wouldn't.

"Do you want to take out your reading book, Princess Julia?"

"Nnyo."

"Would you turn to page 237 in your history book."

"Nnyo."

"Can you tell me what 27 minus 5 is?"

"Nnyo."

Teachers were hired and fired – either because they couldn't teach Julia any of her lessons or because they would complain about Julia's rudeness. (It's kind of a rule that unless you actually are royalty, you're not allowed to say anything bad about royalty – not if you want to keep your job.) So what happened was that the Princess got more and more spoiled and more and more annoying and more and more... well... let's just say that she wasn't learning as quickly as her parents would have liked. And her parents really didn't like it. They were getting worried that Julia would end up being... umm... well, not smart.

Still, they didn't know what to do. They tried punishing her but she was so headstrong she'd outlast them. For example, they would send her to bed without her supper because she'd refuse to read her book, and she'd not only skip dinner but breakfast as well and by lunch the next day her parents were begging her to eat something. They'd send her to her room for being rude, and she'd stay there for days, refusing to come out. They'd take away her favorite toy and she'd throw all of her other toys out the window just to spite them. The King and Queen were about to give up on her completely and resign themselves to the fact that their daughter was going to grow up to be a mean, spoiled, stu-... er... not very smart Princess.

Two things happened to Julia that changed everything and may have even saved the kingdom. (Because one day Julia would have become Queen. Yikes!)

The first thing wasn't really a "thing", it was a person (actually both things were people but we haven't gotten to that yet). The King's wisest counselor was actually a woman – which was really unusual a long time ago because men always used to be in charge and tell women what to do. (Can you imagine?)

This counselor was Julia's Aunt Serene, her mom's sister. The King had always been impressed by how smart the Queen was (it was one of the reasons he fell in love with her) but her sister was even smarter. After years of listening to his advisors tell him one thing and then having Aunt Serene give him much better advice over dinner or tea he finally just made her his chief counselor. Aunt Serene had watched her sister and the King suffer with Julia's behavior for years and felt for them, but everyone knows that you are not supposed to give parents advice about how to raise their kids (even if they aren't Kings and Queens) – not unless you want to be hated for the rest of your life. So, she kept quiet.

But one day the King turned to her and said, "I don't know what to do, Serene. Is there any way you could help my daughter?" Serene took a moment to think about it and then said, "Yes, I believe I can." And here's what she did.

She never asked the Princess a question. She never said, "Would you open your book to page blah-blah-blah?" or "Can you tell me the name of the King who fought in the war of blah-blah-blah? " She didn't even give Julia orders that she could say "No" to, like, "Read chapters twenty-one through twenty-five." She started by just reading out loud. She'd lock the door to the library where Julia was supposed to take her lessons and she'd just read her own favorite books out loud. At first the Princess tried to fight it – she'd go off into a corner, she'd cover her ears, she'd yell out, "La la la la la la la, I can't hear you," as loud as she could. Serene just kept on reading. It turns out she was just as headstrong as her niece. Serene kept on reading and reading and reading, hour after hour after hour. And after a while the Princess started listening and what she heard amazed her; how some of the greatest writers in the world could tell some of the greatest stories, turn a phrase, put together a sentence in the most unexpected way and twiddle with words until they made you laugh out loud; how the histories showed you about people great and small who fought wars, struggled for peace, achieved greatness or faltered in the face of adversity; how mathematicians developed unheard of formulas to help you solve the problems of life; how incredible scientific discoveries saved the lives of millions of people and changed how we look at the world. Julia couldn't get enough and when she asked for more, her Aunt was always ready with more.

Julia was really, really smart as it turns out and she learned fast. She soaked up books and ideas like crazy. Pretty soon the Princess was reading on her own, then reading out loud to Serene, then writing her own stories and solving her own problems. The King was thrilled, the Queen was relieved and Serene… you'd think she'd be proud but she said that being proud would mean that she had something to do with Julia's being so smart – and she didn't. All she did was give her some chances to use the brain she already had. So she was just grateful that she could help. That's what she always said: she was grateful.

No wonder Julia loved her so much. Who wouldn't? Aunt Serene wasn't just her teacher, she was her friend, her only one… so far. Now, having a good friend for the first time and learning all that stuff, you'd think that Julia would have also figured out how to say more than just "No." Well, she did… to her Aunt. But to everyone else it was the same old story. Only now she was older and it wasn't the little girl, pouty, "Nnyo," anymore it was a teenage, spoiled, snobbish, short, "No," as she looked down her nose at you. Sheesh.

The second thing that happened to Julia was a little scarier. It happened because she always said, "No," and because now that she had read so many books, she thought she knew everything and you know what? She didn't.

It was her first time on horseback, and when the stable-hands asked her if she needed help with riding and the royal guards asked her if she needed an escort she, of course, said, "No." So, when a storm came up and her horse got scared by lightening and took off across the countryside she didn't know how to stop. The horse galloped for miles and miles into a deep, dark and rainy wood. She could barely hold on. She lost her crown, had her dress torn and her face and arms cut by the branches flying past her, until she was finally thrown from the horse and landed in a sticker bush and broke her arm.

She started crying from the pain in her arm and all the cuts from the thorns. As hard as it was, she finally got herself free from the bush and pulled most of the stickers out of her arms and legs and tummy and bottom. She realized she must be miles and miles from the castle; she was completely lost and didn't even know which direction to go to get out of the forest. On top of that she was really, really hurting.

It was when she was at her worst-- all scratched up and bloody and crying, sitting in the mud with her hair soaked and stuck with stickers and thorns-- that this Young Man showed up. He was leading the Princess's horse by the reins. He asked Julia if she was okay and she said, "No!" In her head, she thought, "Is he a total idiot? Do I look like I'm okay?" He asked her if she needed some help and again, you know what she said? That's right. She said, "No," and got to her feet, even though it was hard and she was starting to feel woozy from the pain in her arm. She said, "No... no... no..." and she fainted. Just like that.

Most people have never fainted or seen someone faint but it's as if the bones in your body disappear and you just sort of mush to the ground in slow motion. The Young Man hadn't seen anything like it so he didn't move fast enough to catch her and she smacked her head on a stone. He didn't know what to make of this muddy, bloody, broken, crazy girl, so he picked her up and laid her over the horse's back and took her home with him.

When Julia woke up in a harsh straw bed she didn't know where she was. Her broken arm was in a splint and was still pounding with pain, she had bruises all over and ointment on her cuts and scratches. The Princess called out for help but no one came so she screamed her head off in the loudest, shriekiest voice until the Young Man came running into the house. For the first time in her life Julia let loose with a torrent of words, and, as we would expect, none of them were very nice. She demanded to be taken to the castle immediately or, at the very least, have physicians and servants sent for.

The Young Man thought she was nuts and tried to calm her down, saying, "Really, it'll be okay. You just need to rest."

That made the Princess even more upset and in her anger yelled, "No!" as she slammed her broken arm down on the side of the bed.

She had never, ever, never, ever, ever, ever felt so much pain. You probably haven't – not many people have. The pain burned through her arm, up her shoulder, through her whole body until her brain said, "I can't take it. I'm out of here." And, again, she fainted. It's a good thing she did, too, because she would have run out of tears for the hurt she'd inflicted on herself.

The next time Julia woke up she decided that maybe she had better try to be a little calmer. She tried to reason with the Young Man to get him to send word to the castle or find a way to get her back home. Even though he knew she was crazy – a slightly nicer crazy but still, bonkers – he explained that it was harvest time on his farm and he could not leave and that she was in no condition to travel anyway. As days passed and the Princess got stronger the Young Man asked her to help out as best she could with the chores and the picking and storing of vegetables from his garden. Of course she said, "No." The Young Man explained to her that he had very little money and couldn't afford to hire help because he was using up too much of his food and supplies on caring for her so if she didn't help out he would no longer be able feed her. Still, the Princess said, "No," and resigned herself to go without food until the Young Man gave in.

Well, a funny thing happened… he didn't. A meal went by, then another and another… and then a day… and then another day. By the third day the Princess was literally starving. After she'd missed seven meals in a row she couldn't take it anymore. She gathered up her strength, went outside and found the Young Man in the field picking green beans and without a word knelt down beside him. She watched how he carefully separated the beans from the stalk and started doing the same herself. After a while the Young Man handed her some beans to eat and she gratefully gobbled them down. I don't think it was just because she was so hungry – maybe it was – but to her they were the best beans she had ever tasted; so sweet and delicately crunchy and perfect, perfect, perfect. She moaned with pleasure and the biggest, loveliest smile spread across her face. The Young Man looked at her for what he thought was the first time because in his eyes the cuts and bruises on her face faded away and Julia's full beauty hit him smack in the head. He smiled back at her and said, "Good, huh?" And do you know what she said? You do, don't you?

For the very first time in her life, she said, "Yes." And the Young Man believed it was the most beautiful sound he had ever heard. Julia's "Yes" was indeed lovely. It was as if her mouth, her whole being was designed to say "Yes." The word was clear and soft and had just the right amount of "s" to it. Perfect. Plus it seemed to hold a whole world of promise – because after a lifetime of "No" she wasn't just agreeing, she completely and wholeheartedly understood and meant, "Yes." Julia could feel the power of that word as well. She said it again just to feel the strength and the assurance it gave her. It made her laugh out loud, and the laugh – oh my goodness - it was like bells ringing. It was like fairies dancing. It was what laughter was meant to be.

The Young Man went from not really ever truly seeing Julia to falling in love with her within a minute. His lonely heart opened and expanded and embraced everything about this Princess. It was so obvious to him now that Julia truly was a Princess. How had he not seen it before? Julia's own heart opened to him in the same way. She could feel his love pour out onto her and it made her feel warm all over. She had never even thought about love and now, suddenly, she was bathed in it.

Throughout the following weeks and months Julia's life became a series of "Yeses." "Yes, I will stand with you and work beside you." "Yes, I will stay with you as long as you will have me." "Yes, yes, yes, I love you." When Julia said, "Yes" to the one question that the Young Man wanted a "Yes" to more than anything else in the world, he realized that he needed a "Yes" from another person: the King, her father.

They traveled to the castle together so that the Young Man could ask the King for his daughter's hand in marriage.

Now the King and Queen believed in their hearts that they would never see their daughter again so there is no way I can fully describe their joy when they saw the Young Man approaching the castle, leading a horse carrying their beautiful daughter. With tears of immeasurable relief, the King asked Julia, "Is it really you, my daughter?"

Princess Julia leaned her head back and opened up the world with her smile. Then responded with what seemed like another miracle to him, "Yes, Father… Yes."

THE END

The Princess
Who Wouldn't Wake Up

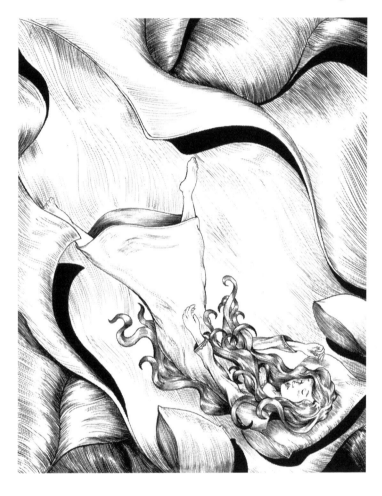

𝒫𝒻

Once upon a time in a perfectly lovely Kingdom, there was a perfectly lovely castle with a perfectly lovely young Princess. Her name was Belle. (Which even kind of means, "lovely.") Princess Belle was not only lovely to look at she was lovely to be around – well, for the most part anyway...

It would seem that a princess would have the most perfect life: she had Nursemaids and Chambermaids, Handmaidens and probably even Footmaidens – everything she could need or want was taken care of. She was bathed and coddled and brushed and pampered; she was adorned in the most beautiful clothing and served the most scrumptious food in the world. BUT, and this was a big "but" for Belle, she also had to work hard at being a Princess. (You wouldn't think that, would you?) Every morning Belle was required to take lessons in singing, sewing, manners, history, religion, dance, playing piano and speaking French – tons of stuff. Every day. (They didn't have weekends or holidays.)

Now, some princesses really hated having to go to all those lessons, and do all that work. Belle didn't mind the work--she liked it. But what she hated--really hated--was waking up early in the morning to do them. It always seemed as if she was in the middle of a lovely dream when her Nurse woke her, and spoiled it. Belle was not a morning person.

She was only six years old when she started begging her Nursemaid to let her "sleep in." She pleaded with her for permission to take her time in the morning.

To be fair, Belle didn't know what it was like not to be a Princess. The only world she knew was this one. She didn't know that almost everyone else in the Kingdom had to work with their hands from before dawn 'til after dark. They mostly had very, very hard lives. She had no idea.

But she did know that in her world, nobody listened to requests from children. And, Princess or not, nobody was going to let her sleep late into the morning. So what Belle decided to do was not so very weird, considering all that.

She decided...not to wake up.

One morning her Nursemaid came in and gently shook the Princess saying, "Belle, darling, it's time to get up." Belle didn't open her eyes and didn't move a muscle. "Princess, you have to bathe and get ready for your lessons," the Nursemaid whispered.

Nothing.

She didn't squeeze her eyes shut. She just didn't open them. Belle didn't move one inch.

The Nursemaid tried a little bit harder, shaking her a bit. "Your Highness. You have to get up," she said, and shook her a little more forcefully. "Belle! That's enough. You have to wake up!"

Nothing.

Now, the Nursemaid got worried. What if there was something wrong? She checked to make sure the Princess was breathing by putting a glass under her nose to see if it would fog up. (They used to call mirrors "glass" because that's what they are really, just glass with the back painted with silver or something reflective.) The Princess was breathing, thank goodness, though still not showing any signs of waking. By now, other servants had come in to prepare her bath and clothing. The Nurse asked them to try to wake Belle. They didn't have any luck either. Next they sent for the Physician. When Belle heard this, she realized that maybe she hadn't thought this thing through. When she first came up with the idea, she figured that the servants would just let her sleep a little longer. She didn't count on this whole drama. When the Physician couldn't wake her and they sent for the Queen. "Oh, no!" Belle thought, "How am I going to get out of this now?" When the Queen couldn't wake her and they sent for the King, Belle almost died inside.

I don't know what you know about Kings but what I know is this: nobody wants to make them mad. It's like your Dad – except he's THE KING!

Now Belle was sure she'd made a huge mistake not thinking this thing all the way through. See, if it was you or me or anyone normal, we'd probably just wake up at some point and say, "Gosh, I don't know what happened, maybe I should stay in bed for awhile until the Physician figures it out." Then you'd be off the hook and you'd get to sleep in some more. A Princess is a very different person. If *she* just woke up she would have to tell the truth. Belle wouldn't even consider lying, not ever. So she was in big trouble. She couldn't see a way out of this mess she'd gotten herself in. She was shaking with fear, at least on the inside. On the outside… she never woke up.

The King came and went, upset and worried. Yelling at the Nurse and the Physician that they had better figure out what was wrong if they knew what was good for them! Still, she never woke up.

The Queen and the servants wailed and worried and fretted the morning away. Still she never woke up. Boy, she hated it, though. She was wide-awake inside and couldn't move a muscle on the outside. She did everything she could think of not to open her eyes: in her head she went through every song she ever knew, then all the poems she'd ever been taught, every dance move, every lesson she'd ever had over and over and over and…

Belle didn't realize she'd fallen asleep until she woke up that night. There was the Nursemaid, asleep in the chair next to her bed with a candle burning on the night table. She looked at her Nurse and thought of how hard the day must've been on the old woman and how she was really her only true friend. Belle didn't know what to do next. She was wide-awake and it was hours before the sun would come up. She wandered out into the Nursemaids room and then out into the dark hallway with only a few distant torches showing her the way. It was really quiet, a little scary, and the stone was cold on her tiny, bare feet. Suddenly she heard voices and ducked into a dark corner.

She listened intently and thought she heard her name being mentioned so she ventured out and followed the voices down stairways and into unfamiliar hallways. The voices seemed to get farther and farther away and she couldn't keep up. She had no idea where she was. She'd never been in this part of the castle. Up ahead there was a light coming from a doorway. She tiptoed toward it and cautiously went inside. Belle found herself in what looked like a "cooking place" (she'd never been to a kitchen before). The huge room smelled of cold meats and live chickens. There was a warm fire though, which was nice. Then she smelled something wonderful and saw a bubbling cauldron of soup cooking. Belle realized that she hadn't eaten all day. She looked around for a bowl, grabbed one and was heading toward the soup when she heard a noise. She scrambled around looking for a place to hide. With barely a moment to spare she ducked into a little cupboard on the floor next to the fireplace. She pulled her nightgown in after her and shut the little door behind her.

The place was small and dark and full of the ashes from the fireplace. She had to hold her nose so that she wouldn't sneeze. There she stayed and watched through the grate of the door as the kitchen help began to fill up the room. She couldn't believe it. The sun hadn't come up fully and all of these people were hard at work and probably had been for hours: little girls - some even younger than herself - on their hands and knees, scrubbing pots, pans and floors; old men lugging loads of firewood and sides of beef as large as they were; everyone working so hard, so early in the morning.

She listened to the cooks and servants gossiping: how so-and-so was sick; how somebody's daughter was out too late; another's horse had died. Then they talked about the goings on in the castle and how she (the Princess) had this strange malady where no one could wake her, like Sleeping Beauty, only no one believed it – they didn't put it past a Royal to fake a sickness to get out of doing her duty.

Then they started cooking. As if the soup wasn't making her stomach growl already. There were pies and meats and fish grilling and baking and frying.

The smells made her mouth water.

Belle was so hungry – starving, compared to how she was usually fed – cold, dirty and sick and tired of hiding and living this lie and breathing in ashes. But she was even more afraid of her father: of the King's disappointment in her. Whatever punishment she was going to suffer didn't seem to mean as much to her anymore – she felt like she deserved it. A King should have a more honest and respectful daughter and these people should have a Princess they could look up to.

She laid her head back in the pile of ashes and cried softly. The tears made little tracks of clean lines down her sooty face.

Then she overheard a servant come running in yelling. Belle sat up so fast she hit her head on the roof of the ashbin. Her cry was lost among the voices in the kitchen but she could feel a trickle of blood dripping down her forehead. The servant was explaining to everyone that the Princess was missing! Even worse, the King blamed the Nursemaid because the girl was taken as the old woman slept! The Nurse was being taken before the King at this very moment!

Belle let out a yell. Everyone stopped and looked as this dirty little thing crawling out of the ash bin screaming, "No, no, no! Take me to the King, now!" she said as they all gathered around her. "Now," she screamed again, and they all started to laugh. She was so angry. She was going to have them all punished; fired – and then she saw her sooty hands, her black feet and filthy nightgown and realized that they had no idea who she was.

"You," she said, pointing to a Servant Girl who looked familiar, "Look at me. Look in my eyes."

Some of the servants laughed even harder, some of them grew silent because there was something in this filthy little girl's manner that frightened them... The Servant Girl wasn't laughing at all. She moved closer and looked down into the Princess's face. "I am Princess Belle. I must see my father the King." The Servant Girl gasped and said to everyone in the kitchen, "It's the Princess."

They all apologized and bowed and hemmed and hawed but Belle was in a hurry - she would have none of it. As nicely as she could, she said, "Thank you all kindly for your service. Now, could you please take me to the King at once."

You should have the seen the little, dirty Princess leading this troupe of servants down the hallways of the castle toward the Great Hall. People were bowing as they passed, the Servant Girl was wiping some of the grime from Belle's face. That face - so determined to help her friend and so scared of her father's disappointment.

When Princess Belle was announced in the Great Hall, the Queen put her hand to her forehead and almost fainted, sighing, "Oh, my goodness."

The King rose from the throne. "What is this!"

The Princess bowed before her father. "Belle? What has happened?" he demanded.

The Princess rose very slowly, swallowed, and in a shaky voice said, "Your Majesty, I beg that you have mercy on my Nursemaid – she has done no wrong. The fault is all mine."

"Yes," he said, urging her on.

"I have not lived up to the honor of being a Princess," she continued, "I have been selfish and dishonest. I have put you, the Queen and many of these hard working people through a difficult time. I pray that you, all of you, forgive me." Belle's head did not bow. She kept it up, looking directly at the King and awaiting her sentence.

The King took a step toward his daughter, trying to keep a stern look on his face. It was difficult watching his perfect little girl covered with blood and dirt standing in front of the entire Court. But he couldn't have been more proud. She was so small and yet it seemed like she was the tallest person in the room. There wasn't a person there – Lords, Ladies and servants alike – who wasn't as proud of Belle as the King and Queen were.

The King gave her an appropriate punishment. She knew she deserved it and accepted it and was better for it.

From that day forward, Belle never complained about waking up too early.

Sometimes she even got up before sunrise, to help out in the kitchen. She became a wonderful cook, a generous and just Queen and, later on in life, more of a morning person.

THE END

The Princess Who Always Said, "Not Today"

PF

Years and years and years ago, in a distant kingdom far up into the mountains there was born a little raven-haired princess with warm brown skin and dark almond eyes. Her name was Marina.

I don't know how the King and Queen could have told what kind of young girl she was going to be, but they got her name exactly right. Marina always dreamed of crossing the seas to distant lands – even as a little girl.

The only stories she would ever listen to were about the sea. The only history she wanted to learn was about the sea. She would beg to be taken to the river, and then sit there for hours, imagining it winding its way down the mountains into the sea. She drew pictures of ships sailing and fish swimming. The King and Queen even had their workers dig a pond on the castle grounds so she could keep her very own fish in it.

The only problem (and it wasn't really a big problem right away) was that the Princess wouldn't have much to do with anything that didn't involve water or the sea or boats, so she'd try to get out of all other things, or at least put them off.

She would say, "Oooh, not today. I'll do it tomorrow." Because she'd learned at a very young age - and she was a really smart little girl when she wanted to be: she knew how to set the sails of a boat, steer it, fix fishing nets; she learned how the winds blew and currents flowed and how to read a compass and steer by the stars at night. She was very sharp - so she'd figured out that if you put something off, a lot of times, people forget about it. Or they would just get tired of asking.

It didn't really seem like a big deal that Marina didn't learn how to sing ("Oh, not today. Let's set up a lesson for next week.") or sew pretty things (just sails for ships), how do dance ("Not today, my ankle hurts.") or ride a horse ("Not today, I think it's going to rain.") or a dozen other things that a Princess is supposed to learn.

It did become a big deal when she got to be a teenager and the King and Queen started to notice how the Knights and Princes who came from other lands didn't pay any attention to Marina at all. As her older sisters found love, got married and went off to live with their husbands, Marina was left behind, still dreaming of the sea.

Her parents didn't know what to do with Marina.

And Marina didn't know if she would ever reach the sea.

One day all of that changed. A young Prince arrived at the castle. He was like no one Marina had ever seen: his hair was long and braided in places and seemed almost wind-swept, his skin was darkened by the sun and his eyes burned bright blue. When Marina first looked into his eyes she thought she saw the ocean in them and fell suddenly, instantly in love.

The King threw a banquet for the Prince. Marina was so excited about talking to him she could barely breathe.

She listened to him tell tales of every waking moment aboard one ship or another traveling to exotic lands, the storms and tempests he weathered and the endless blue skies and starry nights. The Princess almost threw herself at him, shouting, "Take me with you, I'm yours forever!" But she held on.

The Prince, for his part, was mesmerized by her beauty and awestruck by this land-locked girl who could know so much about ships and the sea. They felt they had known each other all of their lives. It was as if she had been traveling with him on the seas, if only in spirit.

So the Prince was really confused when, after dinner, he asked the Princess to sing one of her favorite songs and she said, "Not today, perhaps tomorrow."

He didn't know that she had never taken the time to learn to sing.

And later, when he asked her to dance, her heart sank when she had to tell him, "Not today. Perhaps tomorrow."

It was so sad to watch two people, obviously so much in love, fall farther and farther apart. It was sadder still to see the Prince (who was sure by now that the feelings he had for the Princess were not returned) summon up the courage to try one more time and ask Marina if perhaps they could go for a ride in the morning and she could show him some of this lovely kingdom of hers.

The Princess couldn't even answer. She burst into tears and ran out of the banquet hall and all the way to her bedchamber.

She bolted her bedroom door behind her and would not be comforted by anyone, not even the Queen.

The next morning, even before the sun was up, the Princess was out of bed, determined to make things right. She would not give up on everything she'd ever dreamt of. As she fixed her face and hair she decided to find the Prince and explain to him how foolish she'd been not to tell him that she had never learned to sing, or dance, or ride.

But it was too late. The Prince had been so heartbroken that he couldn't stay in the castle another night. He had gone shortly after Marina ran off to her room.

The news hit Marina as if someone had punched her in the stomach. She had never before felt such pain. All of the air was ripped out of her at once and everything started to spin. As she started to fall, she thought, "Oh, this is what fainting feels li…" and everything went black.

She didn't know where she was when she finally came to. She felt herself moving. She looked up and saw the King's face above her. He was carrying her in his arms.

She told him, "Father, I have to-"

He cut her off, saying, "We're going to find him." Marina looked at her father as if she had never known him. She probably hadn't. "You're going to have to ride a horse, though," he continued, looking down at her, "and it's going to hurt."

It did. The first day on a horse the Princess thought her legs and back and… "you-know-what" would never stop hurting. She was bounced and bruised. She was also amazed that they actually followed the stream down the mountain from the castle just as she imagined. And though she was in constant pain, she smiled because she was finally heading for the sea.

The second day was a bit easier on Marina's behind.

By the third day she rode more capably in spite of the bruises. The stream they had been following had now become a river and up over a hill, below them, Marina saw the sea for the very first time. Her heart rose in her throat.

Then she saw in the distance a ship leaving the dock and her heart sank, because she knew the Prince was on it.

"We're not done yet," she heard her father say as he galloped past her.

The ship was half way out of the bay by the time the King and Marina arrived at the docks. He ordered his men to commandeer a small boat. He and the Princess climbed aboard. "Get her ready to sail. We're going to have to move fast," he said to her as he started raising the sails.

She stared at him. "You're going to have to hurry if we're going to catch him," he yelled. Then, "Where do you think you got it from, your love of the sea? My Marina?"

She smiled and cried and together they got the little sailboat ready and out of the slip. They caught the Prince's ship just before it reached the open sea.

"You be safe, daughter, and come home to us soon."

"I will, father," she said and hugged him tight.

"I charge you, Captain, with the safety of my daughter," the King yelled up as his daughter was brought on board the ship, "or I'll have your head!"

"Aye, Your Majesty," the Captain said.

That's when the Prince came up from below to see why the ship had stopped.

When they saw each other, the Prince and Princess drew the same breath. They wanted to declare their love for each other immediately, hold each other and never let go.

Instead, the Prince simply held out his hand. She took it and he led her to the bow of the ship. There, Marina took in the beauty of the wide, open sea for the first time. She closed her eyes and tasted the salt air as the Prince leaned in and kissed her.

Six months later, as Marina promised her father, she and the Prince returned to the castle, and were married.

It was almost a certainty that they would live happily every after. How could you not be happy doing what you love, in the place you love with the one you love?

Every once in awhile, out on the open sea, the Prince would ask Marina if she wanted to go back home. And you know what she said to him… don't you?

THE END

The Princess Who Hid Under the Covers

PF

Before there were computers, before there were TVs, before there were even radios or planes or cars or trains or machinery of any kind, there was a castle in a Kingdom far, far away.

Ruling the Kingdom were a King and Queen who had many smart young princes and princesses. The youngest of them all was Princess Sarah.

She was certainly the cutest of all of the children. She was also the most playful and fun to be around. The one problem (if you could even call it that) was that she just *hated* leaving her bed.

You couldn't really blame her. You wouldn't, if you had a bed like hers. It was huge. It had four tall bedposts with a lovely, lace canopy over it and curtains hanging down the side. It had dozens of frilly pillows to get lost in or make houses out of. Sarah also kept as many stuffed toys and dolls that she could fit on the bed with her.

If they let her, Sarah could play for hours in the bed: making pillow homes for all of her dolls to live in; laying out tables for them to eat lunch and have tea parties; holding court or having huge wedding ceremonies with lords and ladies, kings and queens. She would stay up as late at night as they would allow her to, playing, and wake up early the next morning to do the same. It was wonderful.

Whenever little Sarah went missing, the servants knew exactly where to find her: behind the curtains of her perfectly perfect bed.

The servants, her patient old Nanny mostly, had a terrible time getting the Princess to say goodnight to all of her dolls and finally go to sleep, and an even worse time imploring her to say goodbye to all of them and get out of the bed every morning.

One morning, Princess Sarah got up early - as she always did - gently woke up every one of her sleeping dollies – as she always did – changed each of them out of their sleeping gowns and into their dresses of the day – as she always did – and was right in the middle of feeding them their morning tea when she heard the heavy door of the outer chamber creak open.

She knew this would be the beginning of saying goodbye to all of her dolly friends and the start of the tedious routine of washing and changing and brushing and eating and lessons and lunching and blah, blah, blah, blah, blah, blah, blah, blah.

So she decided, - not this time!

She squiggled under the heavy covers, grabbing a few downy pillows with her and hid away so that no one could find her.

And guess what? They didn't!

The old, short-sighted Nanny opened the blinds – as she usually did – pulled back the bed-curtains – as she usually did – and yelled out in her sing-song voice, "Rise and shine, Princess Sarah. A new day is dawning and there are adventures to be had."

That never made any sense, Sarah thought to herself, as she surrounded herself with pillows and scrunched her little body down as small as she could under the covers.

"Princess?" she heard the old woman say, kind

of muffled sounding under the loads of lace and frills. "Princess Sarah, where are you?"

She could feel dolls and pillows being moved around and the tops of the huge, downy blankets being pulled aside. Sarah squeezed her eyes tightly, imagining that somehow it might help make her disappear. Then she heard her Nanny, scuffling around the room. "Sarah, darling… Princess Sarah."

The Princess could hear the old woman getting more panicked as she knelt down and searched under the bed and behind the window curtains. "I mean it, young lady. I won't stand for this sort of thing!"

Sarah almost giggled under the covers. She actually did as soon as she heard the shuffling feet of the Nanny head out of the bedroom and out the huge bedchamber door.

She scurried out from under the covers and laughed and laughed. Knowing that her Nanny would be back soon with a servant or two who had better eyes, Sarah grabbed a couple of her favorite dolls and scurried for the giant wardrobe at the back of the room. She climbed in and shut the door behind her. Then she wormed her way to the back of the closet and wrapped herself and her dolls in a large furry coat.

She whispered to her doll-friends that they all must be very, very quiet so as not to get caught.

Moments later she heard the Nanny and what sounded like her older sister, Ginny, come into the bedroom. She couldn't make out what they were saying but she could tell that the entire bed was being dismantled.

If Ginny or the Nanny had really paid attention to Sarah, they would've known that some of her favorite dolls were missing but that's not the kind of thing either of them noticed.

Sarah congratulated herself and the dolls that they were smart enough to escape to this new hiding place.

After more searching and a lot of yelling and maybe even some cursing (although Sarah couldn't tell for sure – she'd never heard any bad words) Ginny and the Nanny left.

The Princess carefully peeked out of the wardrobe and, satisfied that the coast was clear, ran back to bed with her dolls. She gathered up the pillows and other dolls strewn about and pulled the curtains around them, ready to settle in for a morning of playtime.

Well, that didn't last long.

A few minutes later she heard the creaking of the big door again. And again, she scrambled under the covers to hide, grabbing a couple of her dolls.

This time, she could hear that it was two young Chambermaids. "Shoot," she said to herself, because she knew that they'd be cleaning up and she was pretty sure that she was going to be found out.

What she heard the Chambermaids say in between their "Tsk's," and "Oh, my's," shocked the young Princess and made her ears burn. They talked about her being a spoiled young thing. They called her "selfish" and "inconsiderate" and "not at all nice" – which brought tears to little Sarah eyes.

She was about to scream out, "I am too, nice!" when something terrible happened! At once, from either side of the bed, the Chambermaids tightly tucked in the thick blanket covering Sarah so that she couldn't move her arms at all! She was about to yell out when they tucked in the blanket over her face and mouth! She was about to kick her feet, when they did the same to her legs and feet!

Princess Sarah couldn't move at all! And worse, the down cover and all its lace covered her mouth and she could barely breathe! She struggled and struggled and then figured out that all her struggling was only making things worse. With tears in her eyes, she stopped moving - barely able to breathe through the layers of down and blankets, not sure if she was going to die right there – when suddenly she remembered something from somewhere: - that it's always better to relax. You could breathe better if you didn't move too much.

As frightened as she was, that's what Sarah did. She lay very still, sucking what little air she could through the layers of blankets. She waited there for an idea to come to her or for something, anything, to save her life.

For a little girl, she was pretty smart. Because, unlike Ginny and the Nurse, the Chambermaids knew every pillow and every doll that Sarah had. That's why Sarah was pretty sure she'd get caught and that's what probably saved her life.

As the maids were finishing making the bed they both looked around together. They knew immediately that two of Sarah's dolls were missing. They looked at each other at the same time with that look that says, "Something's really wrong."

Sarah *never* took any of her dolls out of the room…

Figuring it out at almost exactly the same second, they tore apart the bed covers and Princess Sarah sucked in the fresh air.

The Chambermaids started crying and apologizing – really afraid for their lives. Could you imagine if they killed the Princess?

The Princess was just as frightened. So much so that her whole body was shaking and she couldn't stop crying.

The three of them huddled and hugged each other and cried and cried until their tears turned to laughter in the sheer joy that Sarah was unharmed.

When the tears were wiped away Sarah told them she was so, so sorry for scaring them so badly.

They became fast friends after that (the Maids were only a few years older than herself). The Princess had them both share her bed for months after that because she was too frightened to sleep alone and especially under the covers.

In fact, her bed was no longer her favorite place to be - you can see why! She did her best to stay in wide-open spaces as much as she could. She learned to ride and visited the farms and villages beyond the castle walls. She spent lazy days with shepherds and goatherds in the green, hilly pastures. She learned to fish and boat in the rivers and streams and even took a voyage across the sea, with her mother, the Queen.

Once she left her world of dolls behind she found real people much more interesting to be around. From poets and historians she heard stories of love, unimaginable creatures and thrilling acts of valor on the battlefield. And nothing in Sarah's bed-ridden experience could compare to an actual high tea with a Queen from a far off kingdom or the soaring emotion of the real, royal wedding of her eldest sister.

In time, Sarah actually gave away some of her

precious dolls: one each to the Chambermaids; and a few more to little girls she felt would truly care for them as she had. (She kept some of them, of course – she wasn't crazy!)

No one would ever call her "selfish" or "inconsiderate" or "not at all nice" anymore. Most people remarked how she was selfless, very considerate and extremely nice.

She still enjoyed playing in her beautiful bed but that became a much smaller part of her life. Instead of hiding under the covers every morning she jumped out of bed ready to start her day, meet new people and learn what she could. She finally understood what her Nurse meant when she said, "...there are adventures to be had."

THE END

The Princess
Who Never Let Go

PF

Growing up in a castle, where everything you want and everything you need is there for you, where everything as far as you can see belongs to you (or will some day because you're a Princess who will become a Queen) sometimes - not always, mind you - but sometimes... can make you a bit spoiled.

That's what it was like for Princess Heather.

She was a lovely little girl with dark, almost black, flowing hair and sparkling green eyes. She lived in possibly the most beautiful castle anyone had ever seen with a mother and father, (the Queen and King) who doted on her. From the moment the King saw Heather's little eyes light up when he gave her a little silver rattle, he decided (in spite of the Queen's objections) that he would give this little Princess everything she desired.

And he did.

You might think, "What could go wrong?" Well, as it turned out, quite a lot... because Heather never let go of anything. That first silver rattle she was given when she was barely old enough to hold it in her pink, pudgy hands - seven years later, she still had it. All of the gifts she was given as a newborn, at each birthday, holiday, celebration; every stuffed toy she saw in a shop window, every jeweled bracelet or tiara that she had to have or she would "just die" - she still had them.

Plus, we are talking about a Princess! She didn't just get a couple of gifts when she was born or at each of her birthdays. Oh, no. Kings and Queens from other lands send Envoys carrying lavish playhouses, dollhouses, even ponies; Lords and Ladies, Counts and Countesses all tried to court favor with the royal family by giving her the biggest stuffed toy, the most elegant dress or the most exquisite piece of jewelry.

This girl had a lot of stuff. What a job it would have been just to keep track of it all. But Heather didn't have to: she had a servant who did. Beatrice was her name. Beatrice had a record of every single thing that the Princess possessed.

You can bet the Princess kept track of that list. You'd think a young girl of seven wouldn't be concerned with that kind of thing, and most likely couldn't even read a list that long, but Heather could. She learned to read just so she would know that even the tiniest, silliest, pinkest, most bedazzled Jill-in-the-Box was accounted for.

Scary, isn't it? But you know what? This might have shown how greedy she was becoming (and she really was: the more she got the more she wanted), but it also showed how smart she was. She learned how to read, write and she even learned math when she was only five years old! How about that?

It's funny… people can learn important things even if it isn't for the best reason. Princess Heather's reason was that she had become greedy and selfish.

Normally, for a Royal, the thing to do was to "re-gift". Not in a, "I don't really want this so I'll re-wrap it and give it to someone else as a present," kind of thing. More like, "I have more than I need. When I grow tired of something or outgrow it my servants can fix it up like new and give it to one of the children of those less fortunate."

The Princess would have none of that. And sadly, because she never shared her things and always wanted more and more, Heather didn't have a lot of friends. None, actually. She had Beatrice. She had the Nursemaids and Handmaidens and Teachers and their children who would play with her when they were ordered to - but they didn't enjoy it, so as soon as they could they would "bow" out of any kind of play date.

The King and Queen saw this, and it almost broke their hearts. So the King did what he had always done to make Heather happy. He gave her more things.

It seems that a situation like this can only get worse. The good thing about this story is that, just as in real life, sometimes things have to get worse before they get better. Here's how they did…

Believe it or not, this gigantic castle was getting too small for all of Heather's things. They were being kept in the royal storage rooms, the royal wine cellars, the royal stables, the royal attic, the royal antechambers (whatever they are), everywhere they could think of. The castle was so full of the Princess' things that at last the King could not take it any more. He'd had enough. A few days before Heather's eighth birthday the King sent word to his daughter that she couldn't accept any more gifts because there was no place to put them.

Well, the Princess was outraged. And by "outraged" I mean she raged out! She threw a tantrum so loud and so extreme that she literally ran through the corridors of the castle shrieking at the top of her lungs. Everyone in the castle was frightened out of their wits. None of this mattered to the King. He had made a decision to (finally) put his foot down.

The problem with putting your foot down is that sometimes you don't see where your foot has landed. It can be messy.

The Queen saw the quarrel as a chance to set things right. First, she asked the King to grant Heather one more birthday of presents but ONLY on the condition that she keep all of them in her room AND that anything that didn't fit would have to be given away.

The King grudgingly agreed and so did Heather. (Her bedchamber was massive and she thought it might be nice to have her newest presents nearby until she convinced her parents to move them).

What neither the King nor Heather realized was that the Queen had outsmarted them both.

The morning of her eighth birthday, while the King looked on in complete shock, Princess Heather threw open the huge window of her bedchamber to see what she thought was the most beautiful sight she could have ever imagined: an endless parade of stuffed animals as large as herself, massive dollhouses and the dolls to go with them, pink ponies, white rabbits, silver doves, dresses and outfits galore! It was as if she couldn't have ever asked for anything more. (While secretly she knew she probably would.)

As the gifts arrived at her bedchamber Heather squealed with delight as Beatrice jotted down each item and the Nursemaid directed the servants where to put all of the sparkling bounty. First along the outer walls, then in the closets, then stacked up on top of each other, then closer and closer to the canopied bed where Heather jumped up and down with joy.

It soon became clear, at first to the Nursemaid, then to Beatrice and finally (in horror) to Princess Heather that her bedchamber would never hold all of the glorious gifts. Her sharp little mind went racing…

To start, she sent for the King and Queen and pleaded with them to allow her to store her presents elsewhere, just for a little while. They reminded her of her agreement and told her she had to stick with it.

Next she begged her Nursemaid and Handmaidens to take some of the gifts to their rooms. But they didn't dare go against the wishes of the King and Queen.

As a last, desperate measure she tried to convince Beatrice to help her sneak some of the larger items down the back staircase to the kitchen until she could devise a plan to keep all of her riches.

Beatrice, although barely a teenager at the time, was a very bright young lady. In spite of the way Heather had treated her through the years, which was with less consideration than she gave to her things, Beatrice truly loved the Princess. Like the Queen, she could see that Heather was a smart girl who just needed to learn a few lessons. And the Queen saw in Beatrice a kindred spirit (someone who was kind of like herself) and had trusted her enough to let Beatrice in on her plan.

So this is what Beatrice told the Princess… "Your Highness, there are thousands of children throughout the kingdom who would think it a dream if you let them keep your gifts in their homes until you're ready to take them back. Most of them have come to the castle to honor your special day. If you asked them personally to do this for you, it would mean the world to them and at the same time solve your problem."

Heather stared at Beatrice for the longest time. We know the Princess was a smart little girl, so no one can say for sure if she figured out the Queen's plan or if she was just desperate for a solution but she finally said, "Let's do it!"

The girls dug their way through the mass of presents to the huge window of the Princess' bedchamber. They opened it and went out on the balcony. Below them, the courtyard was filled with thousands of people who had shown up to celebrate Heather's birthday.

The Princess took a deep breath and yelled to a red-headed little girl in the crowd, "You! What's your name?" The little girl gasped. Shocked that a real Princess should point her out. Her voice was trembling as she answered, "Chloe. Your Highness."

"Chloe," the Princess yelled down, "Keep this for me until I ask for it's return. Can you do that for me?"

Chloe's eyes and mouth dropped open in shock. She shook her head "Yes".

Princess Heather tossed down one the loveliest sequined gowns that anyone had ever seen. It floated through the air above the crowd like an angel dancing and spinning in the wind.

Chloe's father caught the dress and delicately handed it to his daughter. The little girl embraced it as if it was the most precious gift that had ever been given, not forgetting to yell up to Heather, "I will, your Highness. I will cherish it always until you call for it."

For the first time in her young life, Heather saw the joy that a gift can bring to another person. She saw the dream in a young girl's eyes that her own father, the King, had probably seen in her eyes years ago.

She couldn't tell what she was feeling. She looked to Beatrice for an answer without really being sure what the question was. Beatrice just smiled at her.

The Princess turned back to the crowd and pointed to a small boy. "You. You there with the hat."

The young boy could tell the Princess was pointing at him. He started trembling with fear. He took off his hat and bowed. "Y-y-y-yes, y-y-y-y-your Highness," he managed to get out.

"What is your name?"

"R-r-r-... R-r-r-Roger, y-y-y-your Highness," he said.

His mother, beside him, spoke up, "If I may, your Highness. My son, cannot speak clearly but he is a good boy."

"I see," Heather said. She motioned to a Servant holding the reins of a beautiful silver pony she had just received as a present. "Bring the pony."

"Roger," she said, "Will you keep this silver pony for me until I ask you to return it? I will, of course, supply you with the means to keep and feed it."

"It w-w-w-would be my honor, y-y-y-your Highness."

The Princess smiled.

The boy squeezed his hat in his hands and spoke again, "Pardon me, y-y-y-your Highness but may w-w-w-we be allowed to use the pony to till our garden as w-w-w-we had to sell our w-w-w-workhorse last month?"

Princess Heather stared at the boy. Her face seemed both hard and soft at the same time. Her eyes moved to the mountain of gifts spread out in the streets below, then back to the boy. "He has nothing," *she thought.* "They all have nothing." She looked to her room, still jam packed with more presents. There were so many...

Suddenly she felt Beatrice's gentle hand touching her back. It brought her back to the boy. "No," she said finally, "You may not use the pony to till your garden." The crowd grew silent. The boy and his mother bowed their heads thinking they were about to be punished for speaking up. "I will have the stablemen bring you a new workhorse for your fields as my gift to you and your family on this, my birthday. The pony is just for you to… to… it's just for you…"

She couldn't go on. She turned and went into her room and into Beatrice's arms. She was crying and she didn't know why. They both were. "What is happening to me?" she asked between sobs.

Beatrice wiped Heather's tears with a small handkerchief and told her, "You're becoming a real Princess."

Heather looked at her and took in a breath and smiled. "I am?" She did feel different. Changed, somehow. Older, maybe. Nicer, probably. Stronger, definitely. It was maybe the most beautiful feeling Heather had ever known.

She knew at that moment that she would never ask for her things back. She looked around at the over-stuffed room and knew at once that when this chamber and closets were empty of gifts she would go to the royal storerooms, the royal wine cellars, the royal stables, the royal attic, the royal antechambers (whatever they are), everywhere that her old presents were kept until each and every child could experience what it was like to be given an unexpected and unselfish gift.

Armed with this new strength, the Princess returned to the balcony and everyone cheered.

She spent the rest of the day giving out gifts to hundreds of young girls and boys in the crowd below.

The King watched his daughter from afar. He saw the look on Heather's face as she handed out gift after gift to the happy children and he realized that his daughter was indeed a true Princess - whether she had been born to it or not. He also realized what an extraordinarily clever woman his Queen was. The pride he felt that day as a father and husband is seldom matched in the world.

When it was over, Heather and Beatrice hugged each other like sisters who had never known the love of true friendship. They cried together and laughed together and wiped each other's cheeks and cried and laughed some more.

The Queen made her way through the crowd that had gathered in Heather's bedchamber and hugged Heather and Beatrice together. They made a pact that this day would be celebrated every year in the same way with the same love that it spread throughout the land.

THE END

The Princess Who Was Too Scared

PF

A long time ago in a kingdom way, way far away things weren't at all as they are today. This kingdom, like most at that time, didn't have the kind of doctors and nurses that we have now. If you got sick, even from a fever or flu, there was a good chance you wouldn't live. Mothers, even Queens, often died giving birth. Many of the Princes and Princesses died as babies or got sick when they were young and didn't live to be teenagers. In some poor parts of the world, this still happens. But back then, it happened a lot of the time. So Kings and Queens usually tried to have as many children as they could - in the hope that at least one of them would live to grow up.

The King and Queen in our story certainly tried. And sadly, Stephanie's parents – she's the Princess whose story this is – lost all of her brothers and sisters in childbirth or in sickness when they were very young. So, it was no wonder that the King and Queen were overprotective of Stephanie. It was also totally understandable that Stephanie was always scared of what might happen to her. She was scared of a new teacher, a new servant, any new people, spiders, ants, insects of any kind, dogs, cats, horses, storms, what might be under her bed, in her closet or down a dark corridor.

Now, there are lots of ways you can deal with fear: you can run away; you can build walls of protection to keep whatever you're afraid of away from you; as a child you can hide behind your parents.

You can also be afraid but face things anyway. Usually the last way is the only one that's good for you and, usually, it's the one that nobody chooses.

What the King and Queen did to try and help their frightened little girl was to put guards around her... three of them. The guards showed up every morning, fully armed, and they were with Stephanie all day. Everywhere she walked there was one Guard in front, one in back and one alongside her. Before she went through a door, a Guard would go ahead of her into the room and make sure it was safe. Before she met new people the Guards would check them out, search them and make sure they were okay. When there was a storm, the Guards would stay with her in the room, even when she was sleeping in bed! It was crazy.

When an Ambassador or Prince or Knight from another land would visit the castle they couldn't believe it. Why did this little girl have Guards around her all the time? Were enemies really out to get her? They couldn't understand it. It made them nervous, so no one ever stayed very long.

The thing is, this kind of reaction – trying to protect somebody from an unreasonable fear - at first, it sounds like a good idea. You're worried that your only child might get hurt or that she might be so terrified that she'd get ill or worry herself to death so you give her some extra protection for a little while. The King and Queen thought that sooner or later Stephanie would grow stronger, braver – she'd grow out of this thing and they could go on with their lives. That's not what happened... in fact, it was the opposite.

Princess Stephanie just got more and more

terrified of life. She thought, "Well, if my own parents are putting guards around me, then there really must be something to be scared of." Day after day, week after week, nothing scary ever happened but the guards kept their watch so the Princess got more and more worried that something really awful was just around the corner. Stephanie worked herself up into such a state that she couldn't even sleep. She was literally shaking all the time. She had dark circles under eyes and she was biting her fingernails. She was doing exactly what her parents feared the most. She was scaring herself to death. That happens sometimes: people get so afraid of something that they spend their lives running from it and end up running right into it.

It was terrible to watch. Everyone's heart went out to the poor little Princess. It was much worse for the King and Queen. Now they were even more afraid: afraid to take the Guards away because Stephanie might totally break down, - and afraid that leaving the Guards there was slowly killing her. They didn't know what to do. They sought the advice of counselors, friends, even the servants (who couldn't or wouldn't dare make a suggestion in case things got worse and then they'd be responsible for the death of the Princess!). No one knew what to do. No one could help. No one did.

Instead, Fate stepped in. Do you know what "fate" is? It's life. Life keeps happening no matter what your problems are. Life doesn't care what you're going through – it just keeps going.

What happened was, the Queen became pregnant. The King stopped thinking about Stephanie's fears. He went to his daughter's bedchamber, woke her up from a fitful sleep and told her right out, "Daughter, I know you're scared but right now your mother is even more afraid. She's pregnant and she's frightened that she might lose another baby." Stephanie gasped and put her hands to her face. The King went on, "I don't have anyone else to turn to. Will you help her, please?" He could see that Stephanie couldn't answer right away, so he kissed her on her forehead and left her alone to think.

The Princess sat up in her bed for hours, shaking. She didn't think she could live with the fear of losing another baby brother or sister. How could she stand it? She thought of that poor little baby and her poor mother...

When she woke the next morning something was different. Everything in her room even looked a little different. She couldn't figure out what it was. Then she realized that she had actually slept. Then she realized that she wasn't shaking. She didn't have time to figure out why. She had something to do. She wanted to get to her mother, the Queen. She got dressed and ran down the hallway to the Queen's bedchamber, forgetting completely about her Guards who had to run to keep up with her. Stephanie jumped into bed with her mother and hugged her for dear life and they cried together. Stephanie, out of fear of what might happen, the Queen, out of joy at having her daughter in her arms again.

Princess Stephanie never looked back after that. She thought the only way to save her mother and the little Prince or Princess growing inside of her was to make sure that they made it through childbirth. She decided that she would learn everything she could on the subject. She talked to every physician, nursemaid and anyone she could find who knew about pregnancy or giving birth. She even reached out to other kingdoms – as far as she could – to get help from other physicians and experts. The King helped her. He brought all the experts to the castle and they spent weeks exchanging stories and ideas on how to best protect a woman and her baby at birthing time. Because she was always so busy, Stephanie barely noticed how her life had changed.

The Guards, who used to spend their days protecting her, had a hard time just keeping up with her. They accompanied her into towns and villages to talk to anyone and everyone who had some helpful experience. She gave them errands to run, books to track down, specific foods, herbs and medicines to acquire. In time, they even stopped wearing their armor and became more like male nurses.

By the time the Queen was ready to deliver, the Princess and her group had put together a book on the best way to care for an expectant mother and newborn baby and the safest way to deliver a child. The Queen had the best care in the world at that time. Stephanie stayed with her mother during the whole birthing process, holding her hand, wiping her forehead with a cool cloth and helping the physicians bring a beautiful baby boy into the world.

Luckily the Prince grew up to be a strong, healthy, young man. I say, "luckily" because luck still has a lot to do with it – even when you do everything right. Then again, being prepared and smart has a lot to do with being lucky.

Stephanie devoted the rest of her life to helping mothers bring healthy babies into the world.

The King helped her establish a birthing clinic for everyone in the kingdom. Doctors came from all over the world to work with Stephanie and learn from her.

The Princess did her best to be at a young mother's side when they were delivering.

Many times they'd look up at her strong and giving face and whisper, "I'm scared." "Of course you are," she'd say, "because you're smart. Fear is a gift we're given to help us survive. It's what brought you here, to the best place you can be. It's what brought me here to help you. So we'll both be afraid... and we'll do it anyway."

THE END

The Princess
Who Never Spoke

$\mathcal{PF}$

You should have heard the laughter that came from Princess Marissa when she was just a baby. The giggles and shrieks of joy filled the hallways of the castle and made the King smile even in the middle of important meetings in his council chamber. He knew that his young Queen was tickling his new baby girl and could see in his mind the joy that flowed from those perfect, cherubic little lips.

You should have heard the singing that came from young Princess Marissa when she was barely 4 years old as she and her mother, the Queen, danced through the hallways and corridors of the castle.

But I hope you never have to hear the silence that fell upon the entire kingdom when the Queen passed away while trying to give birth to a new baby brother to the Princess. No one could explain to little Marissa why such a terrible thing should happen. No one could comfort the King... except his little girl.

The Princess was so very sad for herself but even more so for her heartbroken father. The only relief he felt was when he would wrap the little Princess in his arms and rest his head in the soft, red curls of her hair. Not knowing what to do or what to say to ease his pain, one night she reached up to his sad face and touched it with her soft, white hand whispering to him, "I miss mommy, too... and I didn't really need a little brother."

At once Marissa knew she had made a horrible, horrible mistake. The King gasped as if he had been stabbed with a knife. She could see in his eyes what had happened: he had been so destroyed by the loss of the Queen that he hadn't even realized that his future Prince had died as well.

The King almost dropped the Princess from his arms. He was struck with so much pain, so quickly that he clutched at his heart in case it might break apart inside his chest. He let out a moan so deep that Marissa felt it in the bottom of her stomach. She cried out to him, "I'm sorry. I'm sorry, I'm so sorry," as he stumbled out the door weeping and sobbing.

The little Princess thought her tears would never end. Day after day after day she wept without stopping. How could she have hurt her father so? Why had she opened her mouth? How could she ever take it back?

Maybe there are only so many tears a young girl's body can create before it runs out. I don't know. But after four days, the tears finally stopped. Marissa seemed to take a breath for the first time in what felt like forever and sighed a sigh that finally allowed her heart to rest.

Now, grief can do different things to different people. Some people feel like they have to punish someone else for the pain they've gone through. Some hold onto the hurt long after it's gone and make it part of their lives. Some refuse to get close to anyone ever again because they're afraid they might be hurt. That's what the King did: he withdrew from anyone and everyone, including his daughter.

Marissa didn't do any of these things. She decided that she would ease the pain of anyone and everyone she could; however she could.

She didn't want to hurt anyone ever again.

The young Princess decided that she would

never say another word that might hurt another person. Then she thought, "Wait… how would I know for sure?" Then she thought, "Maybe it would be better to never speak again."

So she tried it. What happened in the days and weeks after convinced her that's exactly what she should do.

The Princess decided that she would take an active role in helping people so she would wander through the castle seeing who and where she could lend a hand. She'd help the Nursemaids in the nursery, the Stable Boys in the stables, the Kitchenmaids in the kitchen and the Scullerymaids in the… scullery, I guess – whatever that is.

Wherever she saw someone having a hard time she tried to help. It drove her handmaidens and teachers crazy at first but Marissa was so sweet and giving it was almost impossible to be upset with her.

Whenever she helped she didn't speak a word. The surprising thing was – no one spoke to her. That gave her the idea that maybe people who do good for others just don't talk about it.

Now, that might be true but what the Princess didn't know (and this was something that's not really great about those times and that kingdom but it was pretty much true) is that you aren't allowed to talk to royalty unless they talk to you first. Since the Princess didn't say anything, neither could the person she was helping.

It also became clear to Marissa that the more she didn't talk, the more she learned…

First she learned that when you're quiet, after awhile people forget about you and talk to each other, almost as if you're not there. So you find out all sorts or stuff that servants would never say out loud – not to a Princess, especially! Details about their family: who's sick, injured, crazy, marrying or dying; things about their jobs and gossip about the castle; even really fun stuff like who's kissing who in a dark corridor.

Second, she learned something even more important: most people don't really listen. They might think they do, they may try to, but mostly people are just nodding, waiting for a chance to tell you what they think about whatever it is you're talking about. But if you don't even want to talk - you listen. And when you listen – I mean really, really listen - people see that you care and they tell you what is truly in their soul. They grow to appreciate you like no one else.

Because she listened so well, the Princess ended up holding more hands, wiping away more tears, hugging and laughing with more people in one year than you or I would in our entire lifetimes.

Now one of the problems the Princess had with keeping silent was that she couldn't ask or answer questions and that seemed kind of rude, you know? Plus as Marissa was hearing more of people's stories and secrets she became more curious about their lives and the world around them and was dying to ask them for more details.

She decided that she had to learn to read and write immediately. That might sound hard to do when you don't talk and you're only five years old. But the Princess was a very bright little girl and she had help.

Her first teacher's name was Danielle. Danielle had been looking after the King ever since the Queen passed away. She was very fond of Marissa, and her heart went out to her. She watched as the little

Princess grew silent, she saw her need to help others and her desire to learn to read and write. So Danielle spent every moment she could helping the Princess.

Of course Marissa had to practice her alphabet, learn how to spell words, put together phrases and sentences. She was eager to learn, eager to do these things. But what she most looked forward to was when her teacher read to her, because "Stories are dreams with words," Danielle would tell her.

"There are stories of war to teach courage, strength and sacrifice," she explained. "And there are stories of adventure to teach daring and romance. But these... these are the stories my father read to me when I was very small, and they..." Danielle caught herself as she realized how the thought could hurt Marissa's feelings. It didn't. Marissa touched her teacher's arm and smiled to let her know she wasn't sad.

Danielle pulled the little Princess close and held her as they both sighed a bit, finding a moment of peace. Neither of them had mothers, or the comfort of sisters, but now they had each other. "How can you be so wise at such a young age?" Danielle said, almost to herself. Marissa broke away, excited. She knew the answer to this. She pointed to her mouth, frowned, and shook her head "No," then pointed to her ears and confidently nodded, "Yes." Which made them both laugh. (You can laugh even if you don't talk.)

I don't know if Marissa was just an extremely bright young girl or if not talking sharpened all of Marissa's other senses (the way a blind person's sense of hearing and smell are heightened) but she learned very quickly. She didn't learn everything right away. It was years before she could truly read and write.

Sometimes, as she practiced her writing, the Princess would sit silently in the King's Court while the men would read petitions and proclamations from the great books. She would listen intently to every single word (she was already one of the best listeners, ever) and write down the words she thought she knew. Later, she would track down the book or scroll and compare the words she'd written down.

While in Court Marissa saw how Danielle's father, one of her King's oldest and wisest advisors was constantly being ignored. After a while she figured out why: it was because the Advisor was always telling the King what he "must do." What King would like that? What person would, really? She knew she had to help before the old man lost his job, or worse, his head!

Since what the Princess wanted most in the world was not to cause anyone pain she took great care with each and every word she wrote.

One day Danielle's father felt a little tug on his robe and looked down to see Marissa. She handed the Advisor a note that said: "Sometimes people like to be a part of the decision."

The old man saw the wisdom of her words — even though she was only 10 years old at the time. From then on each time a decision had to be made the Advisor would ask the King what his thoughts were. Then they would talk it over until they came to a decision together. (You know what, it was usually even better than the advice the Advisor would have given the King in the first place.) From then on he again became the Kings most trusted friend.

"All this time, the King rarely spoke to the

Princess It nearly broke her heart, and the hearts of those around her. But Marissa, in her unusual wisdom, understood her father's pain only too well. It was the one thing they had shared, all these years.

She could see that her father's heart was still broken and wanted to help him if she could. She wasn't the only one. People believed that a King should have a family: Princes and Princesses running about; heirs to the throne. Many of the Ladies of the castle, and even Princesses from other Kingdoms came to call, flattered him, wooed him, did anything they could to have him gaze upon them as he had upon Marissa's mother - but it was not to be.

The only one he was ever close to was Danielle. She was there for the King at the darkest days of his grief, tending to him, making sure he ate well, slept and tended to the business of a King. At first she helped him because her father, the Advisor, demanded it, then later out of duty to her King, and finally, out of love and devotion.

Marissa could see the love that Danielle held for her father. In her wise silence, she could feel it. She believed that Danielle was the one for him and that her father would love her in return if he would only let her into his broken heart.

One day the old Advisor stepped up in front of the Court and announced that Princess Marissa would like an audience with the King, her father. Word spread around the castle like wildfire. Everyone knew and loved the Princess and almost no one had heard her speak. On the day, they all flocked to the Court and crowded in to listen.

Marissa rose from her seat in the corner and stood before her father, in front of the whole Court, and very nearly the whole castle:

"Your Highness," she began, "I have chosen not to speak these many years for fear of harming another living soul. But I find that I can no longer allow myself the luxury of fear. I must be brave enough to risk losing my father for a second time and ask the same level of courage from you."

The King's face turned hard. Everyone in the Court took a deep breath. But Marissa swallowed and continued in a stronger voice than before...

"I demand to have a father who is not afraid to love. This kingdom deserves a King with a full heart, open and willing to share with his people."

The King rose from his chair and everyone in the Court bowed, except for the Princess who kept his gaze. He walked slowly to her. His face was as determined as Marissa's. He stood in front of her, towering over the little girl and he slowly drew his long, heavy sword. The Court gasped afraid for the young Princess's life...

They watched as the King's face slowly softened and he knelt before his brave, beautiful daughter. Offering his sword to her, he said in a soft, proud voice: "You should rule this kingdom, Princess. You are far wiser and braver than I."

The Princess quickly held her delicate hand to his lips and whispered, "Ssshhh. Sometimes it is better not to speak."

The King dropped his sword, the two embraced.

The Court erupted with cheers and sighs of relief.

No one there would ever forget this moment.

History books would tell of the Princess Who

Never Spoke. They would go on to tell how the King and Danielle married and had many sons and daughters who all enjoyed the wisest (though not the most talkative) Aunt anyone could ask for. And that Marissa took over the position of Advisor when Danielle's father passed away and continued to guide the next generation of Kings and Queens.

History would write that the Princess fell in love and married, experienced the joy of giving birth and the sorrow of losing her father and friends. That she always chose her words carefully and that her favorite bits of advice were:

"Listen with all of your heart."

"Think before you speak."

And, "Don't talk so much."

THE END

The Princess Who Always Said, "Please"

PF

In a kingdom way across the ocean, long before your great, great, great, great grandparents were born; there lived a young princess. Her hair was long and black and smooth, and her name was Madison.

Princess Madison was an almost perfectly behaved little girl. She did as she was told, went to all of her lessons without complaining, and was respectful of her teachers, her parents and her Nursemaid.

However… she tended to get whatever she wanted. Which made it easier for her to be so agreeable but also made her kind of spoiled.

She was very nice about it all. She always said, "Please."

If she wanted a sweet before breakfast she would say, "Please, Nurse, may I have a sweet?"

"But Princess, you know the rule: no sweets before breakfast."

"Please, just this once? Oh, please?"

"Oh, well, maybe just this one time," said the Nurse.

But it was never 'just this once'. Madison knew that.

She understood adults very well for a six year-old. Adults didn't mind breaking the rules if they believed it was only for one time. They were okay with it as long as you promised it would be 'our little secret' or if you swore you would make it up to them later. As long as you were nice and sweet, Madison learned, and promised people whatever they needed to hear to ease their conscience, you could pretty much get whatever you wanted.

And Madison wanted a horse. Not a cute, little, girly pony. She wanted a full-sized, fiery black stallion for her seventh birthday.

When her father and mother, the King and Queen, said, "No, definitely not!" the Princess almost giggled inside. She knew that as far as grown-ups are concerned, "No" almost never means "No".

She was extra-super-sweet to her parents, bringing them gifts she'd made, food she'd baked; she sang songs for them and recited poetry... She promised them the world: that she would learn to ride on a smaller horse first, she would take extra riding lessons until the groomsmen were sure she could handle a larger horse, she would never, ever ride on her own and never, ever outside the castle walls.

Finally the King and Queen agreed and finally her seventh birthday arrived and Madison was given the most beautiful black horse with a long flowing mane. She love, love, loved it.

Her parents reminded her of all her promises and she immediately re-promised them all. Then, almost as immediately, forgot them.

As soon as she could get away, she found a stable boy to saddle up her horse, give her a few tips on how to ride and off she went, right out of the castle.

I don't know if you've ever ridden a horse but if you don't know what you're doing, it's not that much fun. You get bounced up and down on the saddle and horses are really strong and hard to control. The Princess was getting pretty tired of it pretty fast so she asked the horse to stop.

Do you know what happened? Nothing. She said it again, louder. Nothing. Then she screamed in that annoying, little spoiled-girl shriek, "Stop!" Again, nothing.

She figured the horse must be deaf or something. (And she really didn't appreciate the fact that she got a broken horse for her birthday. She was definitely going to speak to her parents about that.) So, she kicked the horse to get his attention. Which is, of course, the worse thing you could ever do.

The horse took off as fast as he could across the countryside. Princess Madison was bounced high into the air and landed back on the saddle, banging her nose on the horn of the saddle. She hung on for dear life as the horse galloped and blood flowed from her nose all over her face and dress and hair.

She was screaming and crying but the horse didn't care. She yelled, "Please, please, please stop," but the horse still didn't care.

The horse came to a stone wall and leaped over it. The landing was so hard, little Madison couldn't hold on and was thrown into a bush, banged her head and everything went dark…

When the Princess woke up she had no idea of where she was or how she got there. It was nighttime and since there wasn't any electricity back then and no lights, she could barely see. She didn't have the slightest idea of what to do. So, she sat there and cried and cried.

When the crying got kind of boring she decided she'd better get up off the damp ground and see if she could find her way back to the castle. Surely, she thought, the King would have sent out the entire army to find her, so it probably wouldn't be long before she was back home, safe in her bed.

But a seven year-old Princess who's never even been beyond the castle grounds isn't that good a judge of how the world works. Yes, the King's army was out looking for her but they didn't have a clue which direction to take. Plus it was night so they had to use torches to see with and had to move very slowly. It could be days, weeks even, before they found her.

Meanwhile she walked. She walked and walked and walked until her feet hurt. Finally, from the top of a hill, she saw a light. A cottage maybe, she thought, way off in the distance. At least it was some hope. As tired and sore as she was, she found the strength to push herself on.

An Old Man - maybe, like, a hundred years old - opened the door when she knocked. "What?" he demanded when he saw the bloody, scraggly-haired, dirty little girl.

"I... I am Princess Madison. I am hurt and I require your assistance." Then, with a forced smile, she added, "Please."

The Old Man laughed in a raspy, old voice and slammed the door in her face.

Well! She certainly didn't expect this. You should have seen her face. Do you know what "aghast" means? You're shocked like you've never been shocked before. Madison was aghast.

She knocked on the door again, hard, angrily, ready to give this Old Man a piece of her mind. She might even have him beheaded if she felt like it. But the door never opened. Madison was totally confused. She knocked even harder. She kicked it. She even threw her body up against it. Nothing.

She didn't understand. What was going on?

Who was this person? Why had everything in her life gone so horribly wrong? She sat down and cried again.

Then the Old Man shouted through the door, "Ah, go sleep in the barn!" So, the Princess dragged herself to the barn, found some hay to lie on and quickly fell fast asleep.

Madison was startled awake the next morning by the Old Man. "What are you still doing here? Get off my property!"

"Please, let me stay..." she said, "I promise I'll..." but he cut her off.

"'Please?' I don't care for niceties. They don't hold any water with me. And don't make promises to me. I don't know you and doubt very seriously that you'll keep your word. Now, go on, get out of here before I lose my temper."

With tears in her eyes, the little Princess said, "I'll do whatever you ask, sir. I will help in any way I can. I will work. I can cook and, probably, clean. I just need some food and a place to sleep until my father finds me." She couldn't hold back the tears that came streaming out. "I don't know where to go. Please, please, please, I don't know what to do."

Now, the Old Man was mean but he wasn't made of stone. It's just that life had not treated him very well and he was tired of being hurt. So, he said, "Alright. You can stay a couple of days." Then he turned and headed for the house.

"Thank you," she said, through sobs.

"But you're not moving in!" he yelled back.

"Okay," she said as she hurried after him.

"Can you really cook?" he asked her.

"I can," Madison told him, trying to remember

the dishes she made for her parents whenever she wanted to win them over. (From what she could recall, they were mostly sweets.)

"Can you clean?" he barked at her.

"I... I can learn. I'm a fast learner," she said - which was true. She waited for him to say something more, anything, but the Old Man just kept walking and she followed him into the house.

The inside of the house was an awful mess. Madison literally gasped when she saw it: dirt and cobwebs everywhere; bugs and spiders; raggedy furniture, raggedy curtains and a raggedy old dog asleep in the corner who barely looked up when they entered. "Well, start cleaning," the Old Man said as he put on his jacket. He put a hard piece of bread in his pocket and headed out the door. The raggedy old dog followed.

Madison's first thought was to sit down in the middle of the floor and cry but it was so filthy she couldn't bring herself to do it. Her second thought was to leave right then and take her chances out in the country, walking over hills and mountains, through the forest with the wild animals and bears and snakes and... No, she couldn't do that either. Her third idea was to just get to work, and that's what she did.

I can tell you that cleaning that disgusting, old house was really, really hard. Luckily, the Princess remembered something her father, the King, had told her: "When you're faced with a monumental task, break it down into pieces small enough to manage and do one thing at a time." That's what she did. First she cleaned the kitchen sink, then a window, another and another, a closet, the fireplace and on and on as hours turned to days.

Because the Old Man didn't have a horse or any means of getting around, the Princess had no way to get word to her parents. So there she stayed as days rolled into weeks.

Each day the Old Man would leave the house in the morning to work in the fields, tend the cows and feed the chickens. He would bring home vegetables, game or fowl for Madison to clean and cook.

Each night the Princess would tell the Old Man stories about life in the castle: how she was waited on hand and foot; the extravagant balls she attended; or how each of her birthdays was celebrated from morning till night with dozens of gifts and mountains of candies and cakes. The Old Man listened and smiled, delighted that this little girl had such a vivid imagination.

Over time, Madison learned that the Old Man had had a very hard life. He'd lost all of his family to illness - first his wife, then his son, then his precious little girl. He had to work this farm all by himself. He was lonely and old and his body was always in pain.

One day, Madison looked around the house and realized that the whole place was clean. She felt strong inside. She had done it all on her own. And now it was a real home as she guessed it had been when the Old Man's family was still alive.

Just then, there was a knock on the door. It was one of the King's soldiers, asking if they'd seen or heard anything about the missing princess. Madison was a little sad to tell him, "I am she."

It's almost impossible to imagine the pain that a parent goes through when they lose a son or a daughter. But if you could, just imagine the joy that would come from finding their child again. The King and Queen's hearts nearly exploded when the Princess rode in on the Soldier's horse with the Old Man close behind.

As grateful as the King was to have his daughter back, he told her, "You will be confined to the castle for years to come and never be given special treatment."

Madison looked at her father. She wasn't afraid at all. She, nodded, accepting the punishment with grace and humility, knowing the suffering she had caused. She was just so happy to be home. "Thank you, your Majesty," she said before she fell on her parents with hugs and kisses and tears of joy.

Madison introduced them to the Old Man who, they insisted, would come to live at the castle.

I can't say for certain that they all lived "happily ever after" but they did have a really good life. The King and Queen made sure that they, along with all of Madison's teachers and caregivers, stuck to any rules or limits that were given to the Princess.

Madison *almost* never got out of doing what she was supposed to.

The Old Man flourished under the care and love of the Princess and her family. He lived to a very old age.

Near the end of his life, as he grew frailer and sicker, Madison would sit by his side day and night and tell him stories as she had years before in his old farmhouse. One evening as the sun was setting she felt him squeeze her hand. "It's time," he told her.

With tears in her eyes she smiled at him and asked, "May I give you a kiss?"

"Please," he said. And he closed his eyes for the last time with the feel of her lips on his forehead.

THE END

The Princess Who Grunted

PF

Long ago and far away there was a jeweled castle in a desert kingdom. There a little Princess was born, with the most beautiful brown skin and the deepest black eyes you've ever seen.

She was a happy baby and the King and Queen thanked the powers that be because they were so blessed.

When Maleeka, that was the Princess's name, was three years old she got a terrible fever, which was very dangerous back then. For days and days, Physicians worked on her. The King and Queen worried and prayed as their beloved child coughed through the days and nights. Finally her fever broke and they had their little girl back.

When parents get a scare like that they usually become very protective. The King and Queen did, so afterwards, Maleeka hardly ever left the castle. She had everything she wanted except that she wasn't allowed to visit the world she'd heard so much about and could see out of her window. Year after year, she begged and pleaded with the King and Queen to let her go on a caravan into the desert or all the way to the sea, but they refused.

It was when the Princess was nearly ten years old that it first happened. Maleeka was trying to convince her Professor that the only way for her to really understand the geography of their kingdom was to see it for herself. As usual, the Professor had to say no. This time something strange happened. Maleeka grunted. It was almost like a growl. It was a strange sound to come out of a cute little girl.

She wasn't even aware that she had made a noise, so the Professor thought that maybe the sound had come from somewhere else and he didn't say anything. As he went on explaining why the Princess was not allowed out of the castle grounds, she did it again.

This time the Princess heard herself make the sound and covered her mouth with both of her hands.

"Your Highness!" said the Professor. "I don't believe that was called for!"

She was so embarrassed that she ran out of the room.

When it happened again the next morning as her Nurse woke her up Maleeka got really frightened. Then, that night at dinner in front of the King and Queen, she overheard the Professor telling them about her growling and she heard the sound come out of her again! In front of the whole Court! Maleeka was so ashamed that she ran straight to her bedchamber and refused to come out or see anyone.

She cried and cried. What was wrong with her? She just could not control this grunting. It made her sound like an animal – very unladylike and definitely not Princess-like. Was she doomed to growl like some dog whenever she didn't like something? It was terrible, terrible, terrible!

Who wants a person around who grunts every time they aren't happy? Nobody would be her friend. Nobody would ever want to be around her. Certainly nobody would ever marry her! What was she going to do?

Then she thought: maybe she could just be

happy with everything in her life and then she'd have nothing to growl about. So, that's what the Princess tried. Every day, every hour Maleeka was constantly aware of everything that everyone said and did and she made sure that she was really happy about it – even when someone told her that she couldn't do something or couldn't have something she really wanted. It took all of her strength and concentration not to get upset when she was told (once again!) that she couldn't leave the castle walls. That was the hardest. But she did it.

It's funny, when you try really hard to be nice all of the time, after a while you actually are nice. And people notice. Every time you walk into a room, everyone smiles because they know that you're only going to have nice things to say. They know you'll have a positive attitude and go out of your way to make things go well. It's a really good feeling.

So, the Princess was feeling great about her life. No grunting or growling. Her teachers and servants and Courtiers and especially her parents loved to have her around. She even started to forget about leaving the castle – it turned into such a nice place to be.

Then it happened again. Just like when her Nurse woke her up that morning. Exactly like that. Maleeka was having a wonderful, peaceful sleep when her Nurse shook her lightly and said, "Good morning, Princess, 'time to get up."

And she grunted.

Even before she was fully awake, Maleeka could hear her Nurse gasp. "I'm so sorry. I'm so sorry. It's not me. I didn't mean it," she cried.

Actually, the Nurse wasn't that upset – not as

much as the Princess was - and she really was. She'd worked so hard and so long to be a better person and get rid of this awful thing.

It was then that the Princess decided she couldn't stay.

I know most people don't make huge decisions like that. Like, "I made a noise so I'm going to run away" at the spur of the moment, but she was young and she was so upset and so disappointed in herself and, probably, secretly, she wanted to get out of the castle and see the world.

The next morning, she got up long before the Nurse came to wake her. She snuck by the Nurse, who was sleeping in the outer chamber, and crept down the stone hallways and stairs. She found her way to the stables and "borrowed" a horse blanket to throw over herself and, surprisingly, walked right out of the castle walls.

Maleeka had dreamed of the outside world for so long, she could hardly believe what she saw.

Imagine this: you've been in your house – a huge house, but still, a house – and then you get to walk outside for the first time. No walls, no ceiling, no stone floors.

Outside is the desert: an endless expanse of sand and sun going on forever; hundreds of people and animals carrying fruits and vegetables and meats in carts and on the backs of horses and camels. The sights, smells and open air almost overwhelmed the Princess.

She followed the road from the castle into the small village below and could barely contain her glee. She had to stop herself from helping anyone and everyone in the village: milking or feeding, planting, washing, cooking or selling. She wanted to be involved in everything.

Maleeka was making her way through the village when she heard it.

It was a grunt.

Then another.

She scrambled around through tents and huts until she came upon a young boy who was putting together a birdhouse out of twigs and straw. He was almost weaving the sticks and straw together, twisting and fiddling them into this beautiful work of art. Every time something didn't quite fit together or twisted the wrong way he gave a little grunt of disappointment.

"It's lovely," she said out loud, though she hadn't meant to.

The young boy turned and stared at her for the longest time, not saying a word. It was like he was figuring her out just by her face and voice. The Princess got a little nervous – she'd never had anyone stare at her like that. Most people had to bow before her and lower their eyes. Still, she got used to it and started to stare back at him. She liked this face and after awhile found herself smiling.

The young boy smiled back. His teeth were really white against his brown skin and the dirt on his face. His name was actually Basim, which means, "smiling." He motioned for her to sit with him in the sand, which she did. Then he took her hands in his and showed her how to twist and turn the twigs and straw.

At first she was taken aback that anyone,

especially a poor beggar boy, would be bold enough to touch a Princess. Then she remembered that he didn't know who she really was. Just as she had gotten used to his stare, she soon warmed to his touch, and pretty soon she was helping Basim build birdcages.

When she messed up one of the stitches a little "grunt" slipped out. The boy's eyes nearly popped out of his head. Then he laughed so hard and so loud, falling over into the sand, rolling around, that Maleeka couldn't help but laugh as well.

Right then, the boy's Mother appeared in total shock, with tears in her eyes. "Oh, my goodness," she said reaching out and grabbing him, holding him in her arms. "My Basim." She looked to Maleeka. "He has not laughed for years. Ever since the sickness." She was practically squeezing little Basim to death with love.

"What sickness?" Maleeka asked. You could almost see the wheels turning in her head. "Was it a fever? Coughing? Did he almost die?"

"Yes, yes. He hasn't spoken since or laughed. Just this growling and grunting."

"You must come with me. Both of you." The Princess walked toward the castle, expecting them to follow.

"Excuse me? Who do you think you are?" the boy's Mother said, almost laughing.

"Oh, yes, my apologies," she said and removed the filthy horse blanket from her head. Underneath she wore a beautiful, bejeweled dress and a silver tiara atop her long flowing hair. (You should know that a Princess always dresses up, even when she's running away.) "I am Princess Maleeka. Would you be so kind as to accompany me to the castle?"

Basim and his Mother fell to their knees and bowed their heads. "Your Highness, please forgive us," said the mother.

"No need. I should beg yours, dear lady and sir, I was the one in disguise. Rise and follow me if you please?"

They stood up and cleaned themselves off as best they could.

The Guards at the gate saw the Princess coming and sent out Soldiers to accompany her and her guests all the way into the King's chamber. The King stood before his throne, visibly upset. The Queen did the same but was obviously more relieved than angry. The Princess, Basim and his Mother bowed before them.

"Forgive me, your majesties, for interrupting, and especially for my behavior today," said the Princess. "I am truly sorry for having caused you any undo worry. I should not have run away. I am a Princess and should always remember to behave as one."

"Indeed," the King said.

"I will gladly accept any punishment you wish to assign to me," she went on, "But I beg that you hear me out first." Since the King didn't say he wouldn't, she kept going. "I believe this young man suffered from the same illness as I did as a young child. And it left him with much the same affliction."

The King and Queen looked at Basim. He lowered his eyes to them. His Mother kept her head down but her mouth dropped open in disbelief.

"Although he has not spoken a word since. Or laughed... until today. Which leads me to believe that our physicians may be able to assist us in not only finding a solution to our… vocal outbursts but may even help this young man regain his speech. If you will allow it." With that, the Princess again bowed before her father and mother.

The King raised her from the floor by her little shoulders and said, "That was a brave thing, Maleeka. We will do what we can for you and your new friend."

The Queen joined them and they had a long overdue family hug.

The physicians found that both children had suffered from a strain of desert fever when they were three - an affliction rarely seen at that age - and the infection had never been cleared from their lungs. Now, they merely had to wear a mask over their nose and mouth for several months until their airways healed. When they had healed, and from that time forward, they never uttered another grunt.

In time, the Princess was allowed to travel outside the castle walls and Basim regained his speech. He and his Mother came to live in the castle and he remained a constant friend of Maleeka's.

Everyone in that grand castle could hear them running through the corridors singing and shrieking.

And every once in awhile, usually when they were in the middle of a very serious lesson, Maleeka would let out a little fake "grunt" and send Basim into squeals of laughter.

THE END

The Princess
Who Always Said,
"Hey"

PF

Once upon a time in a Kingdom not that far away, a Princess was born. She was sweet and quiet, with golden, curly locks of hair.

She had this way – even as a baby - of turning her head to the side a bit and squinting at whoever was speaking, with this curious look in her eyes that almost said, "I'm not too sure about you… but I want to hear more before I decide."

The King and Queen worried a little as she got older because Elizabeth - that was her name, Elizabeth - spoke very few words, almost none. In fact, her very first word and her very favorite word was "Hey." It wasn't very princess-like but it seemed to suit her.

She was so quiet that her Nursemaids would sometimes forget she was in the room and just start talking about their daily lives. Occasionally they'd look up and the Princess would be leaning against a pillar with her hands tucked behind her back, staring at them with a little squint in her eyes. She'd nod her head a little and just say, "Hey." The Nursemaids would smile back, thinking to themselves what an odd little thing she was. They'd bring her a new toy and show her how to play with it but after a few minutes they'd forget about her and go on gabbing about the endless dramas of their lives.

As soon as Elizabeth learned to read she started gobbling up books left and right. She loved books on anything and everything: animals, geography, fairies and history - even math. All this reading scared her mother quite a bit. What scared the Queen even more was that Elizabeth squinted a lot when she read and would hold a book really, really close to her face. When the Royal Doctor figured out she needed spectacles (which is what they used to call glasses) the Queen nearly flipped her lid. She didn't want her beautiful daughter wearing some mess of wire and glass that made her eyes bug out of her face. She forbade Elizabeth from ever wearing them.

Elizabeth just quietly waited for all the fuss to die down then went to the doctor on her own, had a pair of glasses made and kept them hidden from her mom.

Through the years Elizabeth got a lot more independent. She would wake before her servants came to dress and feed her and then tear off to different parts of the castle. Some days you'd find her at the door of the kitchen, quietly listening to the cooks, or sitting in the corner of the stables as the grooms would tend to the horses. Other days she'd find an out of the way spot near the armory and listen to the soldiers' *shocking* stories. Always, at some point the cooks or the servants, the soldiers or the grooms, the housemaids or the guards would realize she was there and she'd give a nod of her head and just say, "Hey." And they'd offer a "Your Highness" back to her, feeling nervous or embarrassed about a Princess listening in on their conversations. Then, after awhile, they'd forget about her again and go back to talking.

As she got older a couple of things happened:

The first was that Elizabeth didn't just sit back and watch everyone do their jobs anymore - she helped them. And because she'd watched them all so closely for so long, she was really good at everything - from making beds to cooking, sharpening swords to cleaning animal stalls. She was so helpful and unassuming that people no longer looked at her as if she was an odd duck. They looked at her as if... well, as if she was a friend.

The second thing that happened was that pretty much everything about the Princess seemed to worry the Queen (except for her looks, of course - she was very pretty, with her golden, curly hair flowing down her back). The fact that she seldom spoke, the fact that she always seemed to be missing from meals and parties and ceremonies that she was supposed to attend, the fact that she read too much, danced too little and was always hanging around the servants, simply drove her mother crazy.

Now, the morning of her fourteenth birthday Elizabeth got up before dawn as she usually did, dressed and rushed down the back stairway. When she got to the bottom she found, to her surprise, the King standing there.

"Come with me," he said.

She followed with her head down, hoping against hope that whatever punishment he had in store for her wouldn't be too severe or last too long. The King led her out to the stables where her mother, the Queen, was waiting.

Behind her mom, being led out of the stables was the most beautiful horse she had ever seen in her life. It was a soft, chestnut brown and it moved toward her with grace and dignity, not at all proud, like some other horses. When his huge, soulful eyes met hers, Elizabeth felt they knew each other at once.

"Happy Birthday," the King and Queen said together.

The Princess was touched by the fact that her parents seemed to understand her so well. She turned to them and said, "It is the most perfect gift. Not just the giving of it but the care behind it. I don't have words to thank you enough." And with that she curtsied low to the ground.

The King was overwhelmed and the Queen... The Queen had to turn away to hide her tears from the servants.

The King helped Elizabeth up into the saddle. He tightened the straps, checked the reins, the bit, and made sure her foot was secure in the stirrup (Princesses always rode side saddle). When he started checking everything for a second time, Elizabeth gently took hold of his enormous hand and gave it the softest kiss, assuring him, "I will not cause you concern, Father. I will not."

He shook his head, smiling, knowing a teenage girl was the definition of worry, but gave the stallion a smack on the flanks anyway, launching his daughter into the outside world.

To the Princess the horse wasn't just a beautiful animal - it was her freedom. It meant that now she could go beyond the walls of the castle. She could go almost anywhere she wanted in the kingdom.

And she did.

The horse became her best friend by far, even though she never gave him a name. She worried that maybe his mom or dad had already given him one and how would she know what it was — she didn't speak horse – she probably wouldn't be able to pronounce it anyway, so...

Elizabeth knew from working in the stables that horses love to be brushed. So that's what she did after every ride, for hours at a time. Sometimes she'd sing as she brushed him - with a voice as clear and pure as you've ever heard.

Once in a while the horse would twist his thick neck around to look at her and Elizabeth would smile back at him, nod and say, "Hey." And the stallion would throw his head back and let out a, "fhummph," which, I guess, was sort of a horsey way of saying, "Hey."

The horse always seemed to know what the Princess wanted: when she wanted to gallop or trot or prance, when to just leave her alone and go chew on some grass, and when she wanted to tear off across the hills as fast as she could with her long hair flowing behind her. He also knew that she loved visiting all of the outlying villages even more than she loved riding with him.

They'd wander into a village together as farmers, hunters, blacksmiths, mothers and wild looking children running with sticks would stare at them as they passed. The Princess would always tilt her head to the side, give a little nod and just say, "Hey."

But Elizabeth didn't really get a chance to watch or help out like she did at the castle because people in the villages were kind of uncomfortable around her. (I mean she was a Princess, after all. It's not like you saw one every day.) So to try to fit in better, as soon as she left the castle grounds she'd change into this dull buckskin outfit one of the stable boys had given her. When that still didn't help she did a really frightening thing... she took scissors to her long, golden locks and cut them all off.

Well, her mother was furious. She screamed and threw things and stomped her feet around the castle. She locked Elizabeth in her room and wouldn't allow her to even visit her horse.

Again Elizabeth waited... knowing that after a while things would go back to the way they were.

And that's just what happened. It took a really long time. But finally, the King managed to convince the Queen that they couldn't keep their daughter locked up forever.

After that the people in the villages pretty much accepted her. They actually liked having her around. She played games with the children, helped the women wash clothes, till the soil, pick vegetables, cook and clean and all the while she got to do what she liked the most: listen to the little details and dramas of people's lives.

One day, when she and the stallion came over a hill, heading toward a village they'd never visited, Elizabeth heard a sound more lovely than she'd ever heard in her life. It was a mandolin (it's like a smaller, prettier-sounding guitar). She'd heard one before, played with other instruments but not like this – not by itself.

She came around the corner of a little wooden hut and saw a handsome young man sitting there, playing a song that she would hold in her heart forever.

When he finished, he turned and looked at her and said, "Hey." Elizabeth nodded and said, "Hey," back.

"'Pretty, huh?" he asked. She nodded again.

The young man looked at the mandolin in his hands. "It was my father's," he said, mostly to himself. "He was killed in the wars when I was young. Sometimes when I play it my mother will smile with tears in her eyes..."

The young man looked back to the Princess. "Would you like to learn?"

Elizabeth smiled. "More than anything," she said.

So, for the next year the young man taught her everything he knew about the mandolin – and she learned very fast. Mostly because she practiced day and night, but also because she loved it so, and when people love what they do they have a special talent for learning.

She would strum late at night sometimes, remembering the young man's fingers on hers, gently guiding her. His hands were rough and calloused from a life of hard labor and yet his touch was so delicate. She could feel his fingers as she played.

After a year the young man said to her, "I don't think there's anything more I can teach you."

"Oh," said Elizabeth. Somehow the thought of that struck her as incredibly sad. "Thank you," she managed to say, surprising herself by putting even those two words together. Then she gave the young man the softest kiss on the cheek that anyone has ever felt, ever. "If there's anything I can do to repay you..."

He knew what to ask for right away. "You could tell me your name," he said.

"It's... it's Beth," she said. Which wasn't a lie. She didn't feel like an Elizabeth anymore - since she'd cut her hair. She was much more of a Beth now.

Then he told her that he was going away. He was of the age where he had to join the army. War was coming and they needed all the young men.

The Princess was now overwhelmed with sadness. She took in a long slow breath and it seemed as though the air itself had tears in it. She hadn't thought about her time with the young man ever coming to an end. Now he was leaving to fight in a war and she might never see him again. She realized how much she cared for him and that her love of music had been tied to him.

As the young man walked away it took all of Beth's strength not to cry...

Then a strange thing happened...

It was almost as if the mandolin started playing by itself. Oh, Beth's fingers were plucking the strings but it didn't feel like it to her. All she felt was numb.

Then she heard herself sing.

The sound of the mandolin and her clear, sad voice was so heartbreaking that almost everyone in the village stopped what they were doing to listen.

It was as if the tiny cracks in her voice as she tried to hold back the tears, worked their way into the listener's hearts and made them wish they could cry for her. Only the young man, alone in his wooden hut, allowed himself to, because he understood how she felt. He felt exactly the same as she did.

From that day on, the Princess sang and played her mandolin wherever she went. People would gather around her and listen and be brought to the edge of tears.

It could have been because she was already upset but it seemed to Beth that the villagers were growing angry. Maybe it was the coming war: their taxes were getting higher and their sons and husbands and fathers were being trained to fight.

She did her best to explain to her father how this war was turning his people against him but the King wouldn't listen. Even when there was talk of revolution he wouldn't listen. Even when his councilors told him that the villagers had armed themselves and would soon be marching toward the castle he wouldn't listen.

Alone in her room one night, Beth made a decision that would change her life --and perhaps the entire kingdom--forever.

The next day she rose before dawn and rode out to meet the army of villagers.

She explained to them that she was the Princess Elizabeth but that she thought of them as her friends and would be honored if she could join them.

As they marched toward the castle together someone came up beside the Princess and said, "Hey."

She turned her head and squinted to find the face of the young man she thought she'd lost forever. "Hey," she said back with a smile that lit up her face, and his, and it seemed like the whole world around them.

Then he said, "Beth..." - it was the first time anyone had ever called her that. It sounded so right coming from his lips - "Would you play something?" he asked, offering her his mandolin.

As she led the villagers toward the castle she played and sang. Not a sad song this time.

It's funny, listening to it, no one was afraid anymore.

As Beth and the army came close to the walls, the guards and soldiers saw her, lowered their weapons and opened the gates. Every soldier knew her and trusted her and would never lay a hand on her, and everyone in the castle knew her and admired her and joined in behind the villagers as they made their way to the King and Queen who waited in the great hall.

Beth knelt before her parents and told them that the villagers were her friends - that they worked very hard for very little and they were tired. Tired of losing people they loved to wars that they didn't understand. They didn't come to fight, just to talk. And she hoped that the King would listen.

She bowed her head and the army and all of the castle guards and soldiers and servants did the same.

I'll tell you, most Kings (and most fathers) don't like to be challenged, they don't like to be told when they're wrong and they usually don't even like to listen but every once in awhile... well, every once in a while a King will see something in his subject or a father will see something in his child that makes him so proud that they don't mind at all. This was one of those times...

Now, I'd like to tell you that everyone lived happily ever after but I don't know if that's really true.

I can tell you that after talking to Beth and the villagers the King decided not to go to war. He even sent the Princess as an envoy to help work out a peaceful settlement with his enemies.

I can tell you that in the towns and villages fathers and sons and brothers came home from the army and taxes were eased some. And that Beth would still come visit them all, play her mandolin and sing happier songs.

I can tell you that the young man and Beth got married, had children and after a while became King and Queen and that they loved each other until they were very old, and that every few years Beth would cut her hair, put on her village clothing and travel to another land. She'd visit towns and villages and castles on her brown stallion (and later, on his colt). And always, as she entered each place, the people would stare at her and she'd tilt her head to the side, nod and say, "Hey."

THE END

PF

For more information go to:
PrincessFables.com

Or contact:
Marc Clark
Seven C's Productions
marc@7csproductions.com
www.7csproductions.com